"Is e
Em

"We're fine,"

When Adam saw his mother, he reached out for her. Carter felt a sense of loss as Adam's hand slipped off his shoulder. For just a moment the emptiness had eased.

But right behind that came the pain.

"Sorry about that," Emma said, setting Adam on the ground, then tousling his hair.

Carter couldn't speak. How could he explain the memories that resurfaced around the boy? It wasn't Adam's fault he was the same age Harry was when he died. But every time Carter saw him, the reminder of his loss plunged into his heart like a knife.

He caught Emma's enigmatic expression. As if trying to puzzle him out.

Don't bother, he wanted to tell her. *It's not worth it.*

But as their gazes caught and meshed, she gave him a careful smile, as if forgiving him his confusion.

He wasn't going to return it. He was also going to look away. But he couldn't.

Books by Carolyne Aarsen

Love Inspired

A Bride at Last
The Cowboy's Bride
†*A Family-Style Christmas*
†*A Mother at Heart*
†*A Family at Last*
A Hero for Kelsey
Twin Blessings
Toward Home
Love Is Patient
A Heart's Refuge
Brought Together by Baby
A Silence in the Heart
Any Man of Mine
Yuletide Homecoming
Finally a Family
A Family for Luke
The Matchmaking Pact
Close to Home
Cattleman's Courtship
Cowboy Daddy
The Baby Promise
**The Rancher's Return*

†*Stealing Home*
**Home to Hartley Creek*

CAROLYNE AARSEN

and her husband, Richard, live on a small ranch in northern Alberta, where they have raised four children and numerous foster children and are still raising cattle. Carolyne crafts her stories in an office with a large west-facing window through which she can watch the changing seasons while struggling to make her words obey.

The Rancher's Return
Carolyne Aarsen

Love Inspired

Recycling programs
for this product may
not exist in your area.

 LOVE INSPIRED BOOKS

ISBN-13: 978-0-373-87693-8

THE RANCHER'S RETURN

Copyright © 2011 by Carolyne Aarsen

www.LoveInspiredBooks.com

Printed in U.S.A.

I will say of the Lord, "He is my refuge
and my fortress, my God, in whom I trust."
—*Psalms* 91:2

To Richard, my partner in joy and sorrow

Chapter One

Coming back to the ranch was harder than he'd thought.

Carter Beck swung his leg over his motorbike and yanked off his helmet. He dragged a hand over his face, calloused hands rasping over the stubble of his cheeks as he looked over the yard.

As his eyes followed the contours of the land, the hills flowing up to the rugged mountains of southern British Columbia, a sense of homesickness flickered deep in his soul. This place had been his home since his mother had moved here, a single mother expecting twins.

He hadn't been back for two years. If it hadn't been for his beloved grandmother's recent heart attack, he would still be away.

Unable to stop himself, his eyes drifted over to the corral. The memories he'd kept at bay since he left crashed into his mind. Right behind them came the wrenching pain and haunting guilt he'd spent the past twenty-three months outrunning.

The whinnying of a horse broke into his dark thoughts and snagged his attention.

A young boy astride a horse broke through the copse

of trees edging the ranch's outbuildings. He held the reins of his horse in both hands, elbows in, wrists cocked.

Just as Carter had taught him.

A wave of dizziness washed over Carter as the horse came closer.

Harry.

Even as he took a step toward the horse and rider, reality followed like ice water through his veins. The young boy wore a white cowboy hat instead of a trucker's cap.

And Carter's son was dead.

A woman astride a horse followed the boy out of the trees. The woman sat relaxed in the saddle, one hand resting on her thigh, her broad-brimmed hat hiding her face, reins held loosely in her other hand. She looked as if she belonged atop a horse, as if she was one with the animal, so easy were her motions as her horse followed the other.

When the woman saw him, she pulled up and dismounted in one fluid motion.

"Can I help you, sir?" she asked, pushing her hat back on her head, her brown eyes frowning at him as she motioned the boy to stop.

Carter felt a tinge of annoyance at her question, spoken with such a cool air. Sir? As if he was some stranger instead of the owner of the ranch she rode across? And who was she?

"Is that your motorbike, sir?" The young boy pulled off his hat, his green eyes intent on Carter's bike. "It's really cool."

His eager voice, his bright eyes, resurrected the memories that lay heavy on Carter's soul. And when the woman lifted the little boy from the saddle and gently stroked his hair back from his face with a loving motion, the weight grew.

"Yeah. It's mine."

"It's so awesome," the boy said, his breathless young voice battering away at Carter's defenses.

Carter's heart stuttered. He even sounded like Harry. Coming back to the place where his son died had been hard enough. Meeting a child the same age Harry was when he died made this even more difficult.

He forced his attention back to the woman. A light breeze picked up a strand of her long, brown hair, and as she tucked it behind her ear he caught sight of her bare left hand. No rings.

She saw him looking at her hand and lifted her chin in the faintest movement of defiance. Then she put her hand on the boy's shoulder, drawing him to her side, as if ready to defend him against anything Carter might have to say. She looked like a protective mare standing guard over her precious colt.

Carter held her gaze and for a moment, as their eyes locked, an indefinable emotion arced between them.

"My name is Carter Beck," he said quietly.

The woman's eyes widened, and he saw recognition in her expression. He caught a trace of sorrow in the softening of her features, in the gentle parting of her lips.

"I imagine you've come to see Nana...Mrs. Beck."

He frowned at her lapse. This unknown woman called his grandmother Nana?

"And you are?" he asked.

"Sorry again," she said, transferring the reins and holding out her hand. "I'm Emma Minton. This is my son, Adam. I help Wade on the ranch here. I work with the horses as well as help him with the cows and anything else that needs doing. But I'm sure you know that," she said with a light laugh that held a note of self-conscious humor.

"Nice to meet you, Emma," he said as he reluctantly

took her hand. "Wade did tell me a while back he was hiring a new ranch hand. I didn't expect…"

"A woman?" Emma lifted her shoulders in a light shrug. "I worked on a ranch all my life. I know my way around horses and cows and fences and haying equipment."

"I'm sure you do. Otherwise, Wade wouldn't have hired you."

Emma angled her head to one side, as if wondering if he was being sarcastic. Then she gave him a quick nod, accepting his answer.

Carter glanced around the yard. "Where is Wade?"

"He and Miranda went to town. She had a doctor's appointment."

"Right. Of course." The last time he'd talked to Wade, his ranch foreman had told him his wife was expecting.

Emma's horse stamped impatiently, and she reached up and stroked his neck. "I should put the horses away. Good to meet you, and I'm sure we'll be seeing you around." Then without a second glance, she turned the horses around, her son trotting alongside her.

"Was that man Mr. Beck? The man who owns the ranch?" Adam's young voice floated back to him.

"Yup. That's who it was," Emma replied.

"So he's the one we have to ask about the acreage?" Adam asked.

Acreage? What acreage? He wanted to call after her to find out what she was talking about. But he was sure his grandmother heard his motorbike come into the yard and would be expecting him.

As he turned toward the house where his grandmother lived, his gaze traced over the land beyond the ranch yard. The hay fields were greener than he had ever seen them. Beyond them he heard the water of Morrisey River splashing over the rocks, heading toward the Elk River. The river kept flowing, a steady source of water for the ranch and a constant reminder of the timelessness of the place.

Five generations of Becks had lived along this river and before that who knows how many generations of his great-great-grandmother Kamiskahk's tribe.

He felt a surprising smile pull at his mouth as other, older memories soothed away the stark ones he'd been outrunning the past two years.

Then, as he walked toward his grandmother's house, he passed the corral. He wasn't going to look, but his eyes, as if they had a will of their own, shifted to the place where the horse waterer had been. The place where his son had drowned.

His heart tripped in his chest and he pushed the memories away, the reminder of his son's death stiffening his resolve to leave this place as soon as he could.

He looked older than the picture Nana Beck had on her mantel, Emma thought, watching Carter stride away. He wore his hair longer, and his eyes were slate-blue instead of gray.

Emma had heard so much about Nana Beck's grandchild, that she felt she knew him personally.

But the tall man with the sad eyes and grim mouth didn't fit with the stories Nana had told her. The man in Nana Beck's stories laughed a lot, smiled all the time and loved his life. This man looked as if he carried the burden of the world on his shoulders. Of course, given what he had lost, Emma wasn't surprised. She felt her own heart quiver at the thought of losing Adam like Carter lost his son.

"Can I feed the other horses some of the carrots?" Adam was asking, breaking into her dark thoughts.

Emma pulled her attention away from Carter.

"Sure you can. Just make sure you don't pull out too many. We have to pick some to bring to Nana Beck." She opened the corral gate and led her horses, Diamond and Dusty, inside, Adam right behind her.

"Are we having supper there?"

Emma shook her head as she tied the horses up. "Nope. Shannon…Miss Beck said she was coming." Since Nana Beck's heart attack, Nana Beck's granddaughter, Shannon, Miranda, the foreman's wife, and Emma all took turns cooking for Nana, making sure she was eating. Today it was Shannon's turn.

"Are you going to talk to that Carter man about the acreage?"

"He just got here, honey. I think I'll give him a day or two." Emma loosened the cinches on Diamond's saddle and eased it off his back. She frowned at the cracking on the skirt of the saddle. She'd have to oil it up again, though she really should buy a new one.

And Adam needed new boots and she needed a new winter coat and she should buy a spare tire for her horse trailer. But she was saving as much as possible to add to what she had left from the sale of her father's ranch.

"Do you think he'll let us have our place?"

Emma frowned, pulling her attention away from the constant nagging concerns and plans of everyday life and back to her son.

"It's not our place, honey." Emma pulled off the saddle blankets, as anticipation flickered through her at her and Adam's plans. "But I do hope to talk to him about it."

Wade Klauer, the foreman, had told her about the old yard site. How it had been a part of another ranch Carter had bought just before his son died. When Wade told her Carter was returning, she'd seen this as her chance to ask him to subdivide the yard site of the property. Maybe, finally, she and her son could have a home of their own.

"I'm going to get some carrots," Adam said, clambering over the corral fence. "And I won't pick too many," he added with an impish grin.

Emma laughed and blew him a kiss and then watched him run across the yard, his boots kicking up little clouds of dust.

He was so precious. And she wanted more than anything to give him a place. A home.

Up until she got pregnant, she'd spent her summers following the rodeo, barrel racing the horses her beloved mother had bought for her. Her winters were spent working wherever she found a job. But after she got pregnant, she was determined to do right by her son. And when Adam's biological father abandoned her, she moved back to her father's ranch and returned to her faith.

A year ago she met Karl and thought she'd found a reason to settle down. A man she could trust to take care of her and her son. A man who also loved ranch and country life.

But when she found him kissing her best friend, Emma ditched him. A few months later, Emma's father died. And in the aftermath, she discovered her father had been secretly gambling, using the ranch for collateral. After the ranch was sold to pay the debts, Emma was left with only a horse trailer, two horses, a pickup truck and enough money for a small down payment on another place.

As Emma drove off the ranch, her dreams and plans for her future in tatters, she knew she couldn't trust any man to take care of her and Adam.

She struggled along, working where she could, finding

a place to live and board her horses. So when she saw an ad for a hired hand at the Rocking K Ranch, close to the town of Hartley Creek, she responded. The job promised a home on the ranch as part of the employment package.

As soon as Emma drove onto the Rocking K, nestled in the greening hills of southeast British Columbia, she was overcome with an immediate sense of homecoming. She knew this was where she wanted to be.

"I got some carrots," Adam called out, scurrying over to the corral, his fists full of bright orange carrots, fronds of green dangling on the ground behind him.

"Looks like you picked half a row," Emma said with an indulgent laugh as she slipped the bridles off Dusty and Diamond.

"Only some," he said with a frown. "There's lots yet." As Adam doled out the carrots to the waiting horses, his laughter drifted back to her over the afternoon air, a carefree, happy sound that warmed her heart.

When Adam was done, Emma climbed over the fence. As they walked back to the garden, she heard the door of Nana Beck's house open. Carter came out carrying a tray, which he laid down on a small glass table on the covered veranda.

He looked up and across the distance. She saw his frown. And it seemed directed at her and Adam.

"What a day to be alive," Nana Beck said, accepting the mug of tea Carter had poured. She settled into her chair on the veranda and eased out a gentle sigh.

"I'm glad you're okay," Carter said quietly, spooning a generous amount of honey into his tea. "Really glad."

"No inheritance for you and your cousins yet," she said with a wink.

"I can wait." He couldn't share her humor. He didn't

want to think that his grandmother could have died while he was working up in the Northwest Territories on that pipeline job. Knowing she was okay eased a huge burden off his shoulders.

She gave him a gentle smile. "So can I." She reached over and covered his hand with hers. "I'm so glad you came home."

"I tried to come as soon as Shannon got hold of me. But I couldn't get out of the camp. We were socked in with rain, and the planes couldn't fly." He gave her a smile, guilt dogging him in spite of her assurances. "So how are you feeling?"

"The doctor said that I seem to be making a good recovery," Nana said, leaning back in her chair, her hands cradling a mug of tea. "He told me that I was lucky that Shannon was with me here on the ranch when I had the heart attack. They caught everything soon enough, so I should be back to normal very soon."

"I'm glad to hear that," Carter said. "I was worried about you."

"Were you? Really?" The faintly accusing note in his grandmother's voice resurrected another kind of guilt.

"I came back because I was worried, and I came as soon as I could." He gave her a careful smile.

"You've been away too long." Her voice held an underlying tone of sympathy he wanted to avoid.

"Only two years," he said, lounging back in his chair. He hoped he achieved the casual and in-control vibe he aimed for. He would need it around his grandmother.

Nana Beck had an innate ability to separate baloney from the truth. Carter knew he would need all his wits about him when he told her that his visit was temporary.

And that he wouldn't be talking about his son.

"Two years is a long time." She spoke quietly, but he

heard the gentle reprimand in her voice. "I know why you stayed away, but I think it's a good thing you're back. I think you need to deal with your loss."

"I'm doing okay, Nana." He took a sip of tea, resting his ankle on his knee, hoping he looked more in control than he felt. He'd spent the past two years putting the past behind him. Moving on.

Then the sound of Adam's voice rang across the yard from the garden.

"So how long have the woman and her boy lived here?" He avoided his grandmother's gaze. He doubted she appreciated the sudden topic switch.

"Emma and Adam have been here about six months," she said, looking over to where Adam kneeled in the dirt of the garden beside his mother, sorting potatoes. Emma's hair, now free from her ponytail, slipped over her face as she bent over to drop potatoes in the pail. He had thought her hair was brown, but the sunlight picked out auburn highlights.

"She's a wonderful girl," his grandmother continued. "Hard worker. Very devoted to her son. She loves being here on the ranch. She grew up on one, worked on her father's ranch before she came here."

Carter dragged his attention back to his grandmother. "I'm sure she's capable, or else Wade wouldn't have hired her."

"She raised her boy without any help," his grandmother went on, obviously warming to her topic. "I believe she even rode the rodeo for a while. Of course, that was before she had her son. She's had her moments, but she's such a strong Christian girl."

Carter's only reply to his grandmother's soliloquy in praise of Emma was an absent nod.

"She's had a difficult life, but you'd never know it. She doesn't complain."

"Life's hard for many people, Nana."

"I know it is. It's been difficult watching my daughters making their mistakes. Your mom coming back here as a single mother—your aunt Denise returning as a divorced woman. Trouble was, they came here to hide. To lick their wounds. Neither have been the best example to your brother and your cousins of where to go when life is hard, as you said. So to remind you I've got something for you." Nana slowly got to her feet. When Carter got up to help her, she waved him off. She walked into the house, and the door fell closed behind her. In the quiet she left behind, Carter heard Adam say something and caught Emma's soft laugh in reply.

He closed his eyes, memories falling over themselves. His son in the yard. Harry's laugh. The way he loved riding horses—

The wham of the door pulled him out of those painful memories. Nana sat down again, her hands resting on a paper-wrapped package lying on her lap.

"Having this heart attack has been like a wake-up call for me in so many ways," she said, her voice subdued and serious. "I feel like I have been given another chance to have some kind of influence in my grandchildren's lives. So, on that note, this is for you." She gave him the package. "I want you to open it up now so I can explain what this is about."

Carter frowned but did as his Nana asked. He unwrapped a Bible. He opened the book, leafing through it as if to show Nana that he appreciated the gesture, when all it did was create another wave of anger with the God the Bible talked about.

He found the inscription page and read it.

"To Carter, from your Nana. To help you find your way back home."

He released a light laugh. Home. Did he even have one anymore? The ranch wasn't home if his son wasn't here.

Losing Sylvia when Harry was born had been hard enough to deal with. He'd been angry with God for taking away his wife so young, so soon. But he'd gotten through that.

But for God to take Harry? When Carter had been working so hard to provide and take care of him?

"There's something else." Nana gave him another small box. "This isn't as significant as the Bible, but I wanted to give this to remind you of your roots and how important they are."

With a puzzled frown, Carter took the jeweler's box and lifted the lid. Nestled inside lay a gold chain. He lifted it up, and his puzzlement grew. Hanging from the chain was a coarse gold nugget in a plain setting. It looked familiar.

Then he glanced at Nana's wrist. Empty.

"Is this one of the charms from your bracelet?" he asked quietly, letting the sun play over the gold nugget.

"Yes. It is." Nana touched it with a forefinger, making it spin in the light.

"But this is a necklace."

"I took the five charms from my bracelet and had each of them made into a necklace. I am giving one to each of the grandchildren."

"But the bracelet came from Grandpa—"

"And the nuggets on the bracelet came from your great-great-grandmother Kamiskahk."

"I brought you potatoes, Nana Beck," Adam called out, running toward them, holding up a pail.

There it was again. The name his son used to address his grandmother coming from the lips of this little boy.

It jarred him in some odd way he couldn't define.

Adam stopped when he saw what Carter held. "Wow, that's so pretty." He dropped his pail on the veranda with a "thunk" and walked toward Carter, his eyes on the necklace Carter still held up. "It sparkles."

In spite of his previous discomfort with the little boy, Carter smiled at the tone of reverence in Adam's voice.

"Gold fever is no respecter of class or age," he said, swinging it back and forth, making it shimmer in the sun.

"Is that a present for Nana Beck?" Adam asked.

"No. It's a present from me to him," Nana said, glancing from Carter to Adam.

"That's silly. Nanas don't give presents to big people."

"You're not the only one I give presents to," Nana Beck said with a smile.

Carter couldn't stop the flush of pain at the thought that his grandmother, who should be giving gifts to his son, was giving them to this little boy.

"Adam, don't bother Nana Beck right now." Emma hurried up the walk to the veranda and pulled gently back on his shoulder. She glanced from Nana to Carter, an apologetic smile on her face. "Sorry to disturb your visit. Adam was a little eager to make his delivery."

"Did you see that pretty necklace that Mr. Carter has?" Adam pointed to the necklace that Carter had laid down on the Bible in his lap. "Is it real gold?"

"Actually, it is," Nana Beck said. "I got it made from a bracelet I used to wear. Did you know the story about the bracelet, Adam?"

"There's a story?" Adam asked, his voice pipingly eager.

Carter looked away. Being around this boy grew harder

each second in his presence. Harry had never heard the story about his Nana's bracelet. The story was part of Harry's legacy and history, and now this little boy, a complete stranger to him, would be hearing it.

"Adam, honey, we should go," Emma said quietly, as if she sensed Carter's pain.

"I want to hear the story," Adam said.

"Stay a moment," Nana Beck urged. "Have some tea."

"No...I don't think..." Emma protested.

"That's silly. Carter, why don't you get Emma a mug, and please bring back a juice box and a bag of gummy snacks for Adam. They're in the cupboard beside the mugs."

Carter gladly made his escape. Once in the kitchen, he rested his clenched hands on the counter, feeling an ache in the cold place in the center of his chest where his heart lay. He drew in a long, steadying breath. This was too hard. Every time Adam spoke, it was a vivid reminder of his own son.

Carter closed his eyes and made himself relax. He had seen boys the age of his son's before.

Just not on the ranch where...

Carter slammed his hands on the counter, then pushed himself straight. He had to get past this. He had to move on.

And how was that supposed to happen as long as he still owned the ranch, a visible reminder of what he had lost?

Chapter Two

"...So August Beck looked across the river and into the eyes of a lovely Kootenai native named Kamiskahk," Nana was saying, telling Emma and Adam the story of the nuggets when Carter returned to the veranda.

Nana Beck shot Carter a quick glance as he set the mug down, poured Emma a cup of tea and gave Adam the juice box and gummies he'd found in Nana's "treat cupboard."

"Thank you, Mr. Carter," Adam said, but the little boy's attention quickly shifted back to Nana.

Emma sat on the floor of the veranda, her back against the pillar, her dark hair pushed away from her face looking at ease.

"Sit down here," he said, setting the chair by her.

She held up her hand, but Carter moved the chair closer and then walked over to the railing beside his grandmother and settled himself on it, listening to the story as familiar to him as his grandmother's face.

"As August courted Kamiskahk, he discovered she had a pouch of gold nuggets that she'd gotten from her father," Nana continued, her eyes bright, warming to the story she loved to tell. "Kamiskahk's father had sworn her to secrecy, telling her that if others found out there was gold in the valley, they would take it over and things would not be good for their people."

"Why not?" Adam carefully opened the pouch of gummies and popped one in his mouth, his eyes wide.

"Because Kamiskahk's father knew how people could be seized by gold fever. So Kamiskahk kept her word, and never told anyone about the gold…except for August. And August was soon filled with gold fever. He left Kamiskahk and went looking. For months he searched, dug and panned, never finding even a trace of the gold. Then, one day, exhausted, cold, hungry and lonely, hunched over a gold pan in an icy creek, he thought of Kamiskahk and the love she held for him. He felt ashamed that he had walked away from her. August put away his shovel and his gold pan and returned to Kamiskahk's village, humbly asking her to take him back. She did, and he never asked about where the nuggets came from again."

While Nana spoke, a gentle smile slipped across Emma's face, and she leaned forward, as if to catch the story better.

Then her eyes slid from Nana to Carter. For a moment their gazes held. Her smile faded away, and he saw the humor in her brown eyes change to sympathy.

He didn't want her to feel sorry for him. He wanted to see her smile again.

"August Beck never did find out where the gold came from. What had become more important was the love August Beck learned to value over gold. He and Kamiskahk settled in this valley and had a son, Able Beck, who got the ranch and the nuggets. Able had a son named Bill Beck. My husband." Nana sat back, a satisfied smile wrinkling her lined cheeks. "I loved the story so much that Bill, my late husband, had the nuggets made into a bracelet for me."

"That's a wonderful story." Emma's voice was quiet, and her gaze slipped to the necklace lying on the Bible. "Is that made from the bracelet?"

Nana Beck picked up the necklace, threading the gold chain through her fingers. "Yes. It is." Her eyes shifted to Carter. "I wanted to give each of my grandchildren a part of that bracelet as a reminder of their heritage."

Emma cleared her throat and set her mug on the table between her and Nana Beck. "Thanks for the tea, but we should go. I promised Miranda I would help her with some sewing."

"Can I stay here, Mom?" Adam asked. "I don't want to sew."

Emma knelt down and cupped his chin in her hand. "I know you don't, but Mr. Carter hasn't seen his nana for a long time, and I'm sure they want to visit alone."

Adam heaved a sigh, and then with a toss of his head he got up. "Bye, Nana Beck," he muttered, picking up his juice box and gummies. He was about to go when Emma nudged him again.

"Thanks for the treats," he said.

"You're welcome," Nana said with an indulgent smile.

As they walked away, Adam gave Carter a wave. Then he followed his mother toward Wade and Miranda's house. Carter's old house.

Carter drew his attention back to his grandmother, who watched him with an indulgent smile. "She's a nice girl, isn't she?" Nana said. "And pretty."

Carter gave his grandmother a smile. "You're not very subtle, Nana."

She waved off his objections. "I'm too old to be subtle. I just had a heart attack. I've got things on my mind. And even though I haven't seen much of you, I know you're not happy."

Carter said nothing to that.

Nana Beck sat back in her chair with a sigh. "I've had a chance to see things differently. That's why I wanted to give you these presents now. In the future, if I'm not here, the nuggets will be a reminder of where you've come from. And the Bible will be a reminder of where you should be going."

Carter got up and set the gold nugget carefully back in the box. "So what am I supposed to do with this?"

"I want you to give it to someone important in your life," his nana said. "Someone who you care deeply about. Someone who is more important than the treasure in this world."

"Thanks for this, Nana. It's a precious keepsake." He snapped the velvet lid shut, then he carefully placed the box on the Bible. "But I don't think I'll be giving it to anyone."

"You never know what life will bring you, Carter, or where God will lead you in the future," Nana said, a quiet note of admonition in her voice.

"Well, I don't like where God has brought me so far," Carter said, looking down at the Bible. "I'm not going to trust God for my future. I'll make my own plans."

He gave Nana a level look, wishing he didn't feel a niggling sense of fear at his outspoken words.

Nana reached over and gently brushed a lock of hair back from his forehead. "Be careful what you say, Carter. I know God is still holding you in His hands."

Carter said nothing to that.

"But I also have something else to tell you," she said quietly, looking past him to the yard and the hills beyond. "I'm moving to town. Shannon has been looking for places for me in Hartley Creek."

"You want to move off the ranch?" he asked, unsure he'd heard her correctly.

"Not really. But Shannon thinks I should be closer to the hospital, and unfortunately I agree."

Carter sat back, absorbing this information. And as he did it was as if a huge weight had fallen off his shoulders. He'd never sell the ranch as long as it was Nana Beck's home. But if she was leaving, then maybe he could too. And with the ranch sold, perhaps he could leave all the painful memories of the past behind.

"So why're you shoeing horses instead of getting Greg Beattie to do your farrier work?" Carter leaned against the sun-warmed wood of the barn, watching his foreman and old friend trimming hooves. Yesterday he had spent most of his day catching up with his grandmother and visiting with his cousin Shannon. It wasn't until today that he had an opportunity to connect with Wade.

Wade pushed his glasses up his nose and then grunted as he grabbed a pair of large clippers. "I like the challenge. And Greg's been getting busier and harder to book. Lots of new acreages, and all the owners have horses." Wade made quick work of clipping the horse's hoof then let the foot down and stretched his back.

Carter swatted a fly and let his eyes drift over the yard. From here he saw everything.

Including the corral where Emma worked with a pair of horses; her son perched on the top rail of the corral fence. Part of him wanted to look away. The ranch held too many painful memories, but the corral held the harshest one of all.

His son, lying lifeless on the ground after Wade had pulled him out of the open stock tank that served as a horse waterer.

When she was pregnant, Sylvia had urged him to get rid of the large tank, saying it was too dangerous. Carter had dismissed her worries with a kiss. He and his brother and cousins had grown up with that tank. On hot days they had sat in it, cooling off in the waist-high water.

He should have…

Carter pushed the memory and guilt away, pain hard on their heels.

"This Emma girl," Carter said, "why did you hire her?"

"I told you I needed to hire another hand to replace that useless character we had before." Wade picked up the horse's hoof again and began working at it with a rasp, getting it ready for a shoe.

"I assumed you were going to hire a guy."

"She had the best qualifications." Wade shrugged. "I hope that's not a problem."

Carter looked over at the corral again. Adam now sat on top of Banjo, and Emma led him around. He heard her voice, though he couldn't make out what she said. Adam laughed and she patted his leg, grinning up at him.

She turned and looked his way, then abruptly turned around.

"It's not a problem if she knows what she's doing," Carter said, turning his attention back to Wade.

"She's good. Really good. Has a great connection with horses, and some unique ideas about pasture management." Wade tapped the horse's hoof. He dropped it again and grabbed a horseshoe from the anvil.

"So what's her story?" Carter asked while Wade nailed down the shoe. "Why would she want to work here?"

"She used to work her daddy's ranch till he gambled it away. Says she loves ranch work, and it shows. She's been a better hand than the guy I had for two weeks before I hired her." He tapped in another nail. "She wants to talk to you about subdividing an acreage off the river property. Says she wants to settle down here."

"Really?" So that's what her son was talking about when he said they had to ask him about the acreage.

"Don't sound so surprised. Some of us love it here," Wade grunted as he tapped in another nail. Then he looked up, a horrified expression on his face. "Sorry. I didn't mean it that way. I know why you've stayed away. Of course being here is hard, and I get that—"

"Can she afford to buy the acreage?" Carter asked, cutting off his friend's apology. He felt rude, but he knew where Wade was headed.

The same place he'd been going for the past year in any of their conversations and communications. The ranch was Carter's home. It was time to come back. To get over what happened.

Trouble was it wasn't so simple. It was difficult enough dealing with the "if onlys" when he was away from the ranch. If only he hadn't gone out on that gather. If only he'd stayed home instead of hiring that babysitter. If only he'd taken better care of his responsibilities, Harry wouldn't have wandered out of the house and climbed on that corral fence. Wouldn't have fallen—

"Depends what you want for it," Wade was saying, breaking into the memories that Carter had kept stifled. "I know you've never been eager to have anyone else living in the valley, but hey, she's single, attractive, and now that you're back—"

"I'm not looking," Carter said, cutting that suggestion off midstream. "And I'm sure there's enough other guys who would be interested in Miss Minton."

Wade shrugged as he clipped off the ends of the nail protruding from the hoof wall. "Been enough of them trying to ask her out since she came here."

"I'm not surprised." Carter heard the squeal of the metal gate between the corrals and watched as Emma pulled the halters off the horses' heads then coiled up the ropes.

He understood why the single men of Hartley Creek and area would be interested. She was pretty and spunky and had a girl-next-door appeal.

"She's a great gal, but she's turned them all down flat. I think she's been burned too many times."

Silence followed his comment. But it was the comfortable silence of old friends. Carter had missed that.

In the past two years Carter had worked as a ranch hand in Northern B.C., a wrangler for a stock contractor in Peace River and, recently, laying pipe for a pipeline in the Territories. That was where he had been when his grandmother had her heart attack.

He never stayed in one place long enough to create a connection or to build a sense of community. Which had suited him just fine.

But standing here, watching Wade work, not talking, just being, he found he missed this place he knew as well as he knew his own face.

Wade looked up at him, as if sensing his melancholy. "Did you miss the place? The work?"

Carter bit his lip, not sure what to say. "I missed parts of it. I missed seeing my family. Nana, the cousins. You and Miranda."

"I missed you too, man," Wade said. To Carter's surprise, he saw the glint of moisture in his friend's eyes.

The sight of Wade's unexpected tears created an answering emotion that he fought to push down. Emotions took over, and he didn't dare go down that road. Not alone, as he was now.

"I couldn't come back, Wade. I couldn't."

"I know, but you're here now."

"You may as well know," Carter said, taking a breath and plunging in, "I'm not coming back here to stay."

Wade frowned, pushing his glasses up his nose. "What? Why not? I thought that was the reason you came back."

"My Nana's heart attack was the main reason I'm here." Carter held his friend's puzzled gaze and steeled himself to the hurt in Wade's voice. "I can't live here. I can't come back. I'm going to sell the place. Sell the Rocking K."

Chapter Three

Emma looked up from her Bible and glanced over at Adam, still sleeping in the bunk across the cabin from her. The morning sun slanted across the bed, a splash of gold.

What was she going to tell him?

Yesterday, after working with Banjo, she had come to get Elijah when Wade was done shoeing him. Then she overheard Carter's determined voice say, "I'm going to sell the place."

If Carter Beck was selling the ranch, would she still have a chance at getting the acreage? For that matter, would she still have a job? Would she and Adam have to move again?

Her questions had fluttered like crows through her mind while, on the other side of the barn, she heard Carter make his plans. He was going into town to list the property. Nana Beck was moving off the ranch. It was time.

Each word fell like an ax blow. She'd prayed so hard to be shown what to do. When she had left her father's ranch, she had made two promises to herself, that she would trust in God to guide her life, and that Adam would always be her first priority when she made her plans.

Coming to Hartley Creek and the Rocking K Ranch fit so well with both. Here she had found work she loved, had found community and, yes, some type of family. Nana Beck had taken her and Adam in and Shannon, Carter's cousin, had become a friend to her.

And Adam. Adam loved the ranch and everything about it. It was as if he blossomed here.

So what was God trying to teach her with this? Why had He brought everything together so well only to take it away?

Sorry, Lord, I don't get what is going on right now, Emma thought, closing her Bible.

Adam stirred on his bed, stretched his arms out, then turned to her, his smile dimpling his still-chubby cheeks. His hair, a tangle of blond, stuck up in all directions. "Hi, Mommy. Is it morning? Is it time to get up yet?"

"That it is." Emma smiled and set her Bible aside. She hadn't slept well and had been awake since five o'clock. She'd been reading, praying, trying to find some guidance and direction for her life.

If nothing came of her plans for the acreage, then it was up to her to figure out her next move. She took another calming breath. *Please, Lord, help me to trust in You alone,* she prayed. *Help me to know that my hope is in You.*

Adam sat up and rubbed his eyes with his knuckles. Then he bounded out of the bed onto the floor, wide awake, ready to go. Emma envied him his energy, his ability to instantly wake up when his eyes opened.

"Am I still coming with you and Wade today?" he asked, pulling his pajama top off over his head. "When you go up to check the cows?"

"I think so. It won't be a long ride." Four days ago she and Wade had planned to take a trip to the upper pastures to check on the grass. Wade wanted to make sure they weren't overgrazing, and she had promised Adam he could come along.

"Here, let me help you with that," she said, handing him a clean T-shirt. "Once you're changed, I want you to go wash your hands and face and get ready for breakfast."

Adam tugged the brown T-shirt over his head and yanked on his blue jeans. "Can we have breakfast with Wade and Miranda? She is making pancakes and said I had to ask if we could eat there."

"But I thought we could have breakfast here." Though she knew plain toast couldn't compete with Miranda's chocolate chip pancakes, Emma treasured her alone time with Adam.

"Mom, please?" Adam drooped his shoulders, his hands clenched together in front of him, the picture of abject sorrow and pleading. "I love, love, love chocolate chip pancakes."

Adam made the best puppy dog eyes of any child she had ever known.

"Okay. But don't ask me tomorrow."

Adam launched himself at her, giving her a huge hug. "I love you, Mommy," he said, his voice muffled against her shirt.

The clutch of her son's small arms around her waist sent a powerful wave of love washing over her. "I love you too, my little guy," she murmured, brushing down his unruly hair with her hand. "Now let's go brush your hair then see if Miranda and Wade are up yet."

Once Adam was cleaned up, they headed out the door and down the wooden steps. According to Wade, they were staying in the cabin that Carter and his grandfather had built for Shannon, Carter's oldest cousin, who lived in Hartley Creek and worked as a nurse.

When their mother died, Garret and Carter moved from the little house they had shared with Noelle Beck into the main house with their grandparents. But the town cousins, Hailey, Naomi and Shannon, came up almost every weekend and for most of the summer to stay at the ranch. Bill Beck, Carter's grandfather, came up with the idea of building a cabin for each of the girls so they could have their own place to stay when they came.

Emma loved the story, and every time she walked up to the trio of cabins nestled against the pine trees, she tried to imagine five cousins spending time together, staying overnight in one of the cabins as a group, probably sharing stories. She felt a twinge of envy for what Carter had, and wondered again how he could simply walk away from all this.

Adam clung to her hand, swinging it as they walked. The sun shone overhead. A few wispy clouds trailed across the blue sky, promising another beautiful day.

"Good morning, Mr. Carter," Adam called out.

Carter stood on the porch of the far cabin, leaning on the railing and nursing a cup of coffee. The fall of dark hair across his face and the whiskers shadowing his lean jaw made it look as if he had just woken up, as well.

Her heart skipped a little at the sight.

Then she caught herself. If she reacted to seeing him, it was because he held her future in his hands. Had nothing to do with his looks, because she wasn't looking. Men were an unnecessary complication she had no desire to bring into her and Adam's life.

"Good morning yourself," Carter said, straightening.

"Did you hear the coyotes last night?" Adam asked. "I heard them, but I think they stayed away."

Carter gave him a nod and then glanced at Emma. For a moment their eyes met and as before, something indefinable thrummed between them—an awareness that created both anticipation and discomfort.

"We're going to have pancakes at Miranda's place," Adam announced. "Are you going to come too?"

Carter's gaze broke away from hers, moving to Adam.

And in that moment Emma caught a look of deep sorrow in the blue of his eyes. His mouth tightened, and she wondered where his thoughts had gone.

"I don't think so," was all he said.

Emma glanced from him to Adam and then made a quick decision. "Honey, why don't you go ahead. I'd like to talk to Mr. Carter."

Thankfully, Adam just nodded. Then with another wave to Carter, he ran across the yard, his feet kicking up clouds of dust.

Emma looked up into Carter's impassive face with its lean, almost harsh lines. She wished she felt more confident. More sure of herself. He didn't know it, but this conversation would determine her future.

"Wade said that I should talk to you about an acreage I'm interested in."

"I don't own an acreage." Carter frowned down at her, and Emma wished she had chosen a different time and place to discuss this with him. Looking up at him placed her at a disadvantage.

"No, you don't, but there's an old yard site on the ranch that you bought before. I know that it's easier to subdivide a yard site than to create a raw acreage. So…I was wondering if you…if you would be willing to subdivide it off. I would be willing to pay the market price. I have some money left from my father's ranch for a down payment. I'd have to move a trailer onto the yard—"

Stop. Now. You're talking too fast, and you're saying

too much. Try to make some sense. Emma bit her lip and braided her fingers together, taking a breath.

"So would you be willing to subdivide it?" she asked.

Carter looked into his coffee cup as he swirled it. "Sorry, Miss Minton. But I'm putting the whole ranch up for sale."

"I…I understand that. I mean, I heard that. But would you be willing to subdivide it before you sell the ranch?"

Carter shook his head. "I've already talked to a real estate agent. The place is listed. I'm sorry, I can't do anything for you."

"I see," was all she managed, each word of his evaporating the faint wisp of hope she had nurtured.

The thought of making other plans was too much to comprehend. Finding this place had been a sheer stroke of luck and grace. Where else could she live and board her horses? Give Adam the easygoing country life she'd grown up with?

She looked up at Carter again, wondering what was going through his mind, wondering if he had told his family about his plans to sell. Nana Beck had told her the history of the place, how the family was so much a part of this ranch. She knew how much Nana and Shannon loved the ranch. How could he ignore all of that?

"What does Nana Beck think of your plans?"

As soon as she blurted out the words, she wished she could bite her tongue. It was none of her business. How many times did she have to remind herself of that?

"I apologize. That was uncalled for," she said quietly. "It's just this place…" She looked around, letting the utter peace that surrounded the property wash over her. "It's so beautiful, and I know it's been in your family a long time. That's rare." She thought of her father and how easily he had disregarded his legacy. How he had disregarded her when his life imploded. Why were men so casual with the blessings God had given them?

"I'm not going to let history dictate my choices," Carter said, taking a final sip of his coffee. He tossed the remains out. "This place means nothing to me anymore."

Carter's reply held a heaviness that underlined the sorrow she'd seen in his eyes. He sounded like a man who had come to a place where there was no other option. She assumed it had to do with losing his son. "I'm sorry about ruining your plans," he added.

Emma gave him a tight smile. "I thought asking was worth a try." She gave a light laugh as if to show him that the dreams she had spun around owning her own place meant as little to her as the coffee he had just tossed out.

He tapped his cup against his thigh, his movements jerky. "I'm also sorry about your job," he said. "Maybe the new owner could hire you."

"Don't worry about me," she said, holding up her hand as if to placate him. "I can take care of myself and my son," she added with more bravado than she felt. "Always have."

How that would happen over the next few weeks, she wasn't sure. But she had to put it in God's hands. She had to trust that somehow, something would come up.

The jangling ring of a phone sounded from the cabin, and Carter glanced back over his shoulder.

"That's my cell phone. I should answer it." Then he was gone.

Well, wasn't that a scintillating conversation. Emma spun around on her heels and strode back to Wade and Miranda's house.

Don't count on men. Don't count on men.

The words pounded through her head in time with her steps.

She would be making her own phone calls this evening. Maybe she could take tomorrow off and go into town to look for a place for her and Adam to stay. Look for a job.

Her steps faltered at the thought, but she suppressed the negatives.

Help me to let go of my fears, Lord. Help me to trust only in You.

"Carter? You won't believe this, but I think I got a buyer for the ranch."

Carter leaned against the wall of his cabin, his hands tightening on his cell phone as the words of the real estate agent sunk in.

"Already? I just talked to you yesterday." He tucked the phone under his chin as he made up the bed. He had turned down Miranda's offer to move into the house, choosing to bunk in Hailey's cabin. If he had known that Emma and her son were staying in Shannon's place, one cabin over, he would have rethought his choice.

Seeing both of them coming out of his cousin's cabin first thing this morning was an unwelcome jolt. He had assumed they were staying in the main house.

"Tell you the truth, I had a guy from Sweden, Jurgen Mallik, who came to town about six months ago, looking for property in the valley," Pete said. "We went touring around and ended up at your place. He loved it and said, as a joke, if the place ever came up he was interested. So when you came in yesterday, I called him. He definitely wants to sign up something immediately. We can do that by fax if you want. He's very excited, very interested and very well financed."

"Wow. That's quick," Carter said, surprised at the lift of panic Pete's words created.

"Quick is what you wanted." Pete was quiet a moment, and in his hesitation Carter heard again all the warnings Pete had given him yesterday. How he shouldn't rush into this. How he had to talk it over with his family. But two years of holding on to the past and waiting was hardly rushing into things. And now that Nana, one of the main reasons he had held on to the ranch, was moving, it was all the incentive he needed to get rid of the place and move on.

"So you're sure none of your cousins are interested?" Pete continued. "Not even your brother, Garret?"

Carter threw the blanket over the bed and sat down, easing out a sigh. "He said no. And he's the only one that can come close to affording it." After talking to Nana Beck yesterday, he'd made some phone calls to his brother and cousins about the ranch.

Garret wasn't interested at all. Their cousin, Naomi, was still dealing with her fiancé's cancer and didn't have enough money. Hailey would have loved to buy the ranch, but she was swimming in student loans and was desperate to pay them off. Furthermore, she knew nothing about running a ranch.

He had expected to get the strongest protest from Shannon, but when he told her his plans, she said she understood. When he asked her what Nana Beck would think, Shannon said that he had to go ahead with his own plans. Nana needed to live in town, closer to a hospital.

Which left Carter with no recourse but to go to Pete and list the property.

"So what's the next move?" Carter asked, dragging his hands over his face.

"I'll need you to come in as soon as possible and sign up a basic agreement for sale. I'll fax a copy to Jurgen, and we'll take it from there."

"Do I need to stick around for all of that?"

"Once you sign the agreement, we can do a lot by email and phone. You don't need to stick around after the initial paperwork, though it might be helpful."

An image of Emma and Adam drifted through his mind, and he shook his head as if to dislodge it. "No. I'll be leaving. The sooner I can get away from here the better."

"Let me know when you can come in to sign, and we'll be well on our way."

"One other thing," Carter said, feeling as if he owed Emma at least this. "There's a woman who works here, Emma Minton."

"Oh, yeah. I know Emma. She's a good-looking gal."

Which made Carter wonder if Pete was one of the guys who had asked her out.

As if that mattered.

"She's asked me about subdividing an acreage off the property for her and her kid. When you talk to Jurgen, could you run it by him? See if he'd be willing to subdivide it?"

Pete sucked his breath through his teeth. "I doubt it. One of the things he liked the best about the property was that he had no close neighbors. But, hey, doesn't hurt to ask."

"Just ask him and let me know." Though he had told Emma he couldn't do anything for her, he still felt he had to at least try. Then Carter said goodbye and tossed the cell phone on the bed as he glanced around the cabin. A poster of a ski hill took up one wall. Two snowboards leaned in one corner of the cabin, both cracked in half. Remnants of Hailey's wilder days when there was no ski run too difficult, no boundary that she respected, no jump she couldn't take.

He knew the other cabins, built by Carter's grandfather for each of his three girl cousins, would hold similar detritus of their lives. Another wave of second thoughts drifted in behind the memories.

Could he sell all this? Could he walk away from the history these cabins and the ranch represented? How many pillow fights had taken place in this very cabin? How many times had he and Garret snuck out of the main house where they lived with their mother to play tricks on the girls sleeping here overnight?

His eyes fell on the Bible his grandmother had given him. On top of that lay the box with the nugget. Two small things, but they carried the weight of history and expectations.

He leaned his elbows on his knees, clasping his hands as he struggled with the memories and the responsibility. He had started working on the ranch when he was only ten years old, driving the bale wagon from the fields to the yard. Over time he graduated to the tractor, and then he started baling, as well.

Together he and his grandfather had ridden miles of fence lines, Papa Bill passing on his wisdom, his knowledge and the history of the ranch.

Regret twisted his gut. Sure he had bought the Rocking K from his grandfather, paying in sweat equity and bank loans, but the ranch was passed on to him. A ranch that had been in the family for four generations.

Could he change his mind? Couldn't he simply let things go on as usual? Would Wade be willing to carry on as a manager, or would he want to have his own place eventually?

For a moment he wished he believed God heard prayers. Because that would be convenient. To ask God for some kind of guidance, some kind of sign.

But his belief in God died two years ago when he watched that small coffin being lowered into the ground, taking his purpose in life with it.

Carter pushed himself to his feet. The decision was made. It was time to move on. Pete had found him a buyer, and that was all the sign he needed. Now all he had to do was tell Wade.

And Nana Beck.

He pulled in a long breath and reminded himself this was the right thing to do. Then he left the cabin.

The sound of laughter greeted him as he pushed open the door of Wade's house.

The first thing he saw was Adam sitting at the table, his cheeks smeared with syrup, forking a piece of pancake into his mouth. Just as his son used to.

The glimmer from the past twisted, and any regrets he had about selling the farm seemed to disappear.

Adam looked up when he came into the kitchen. "Are you going to have pancakes too, Mr. Carter?"

Carter gave him a quick shake of his head, no.

But Miranda was already setting an extra plate on the table. "Of course you're going to join us," Miranda was saying. "I'll even get Emma to make a letter C for you."

Carter glanced over at the stove, where Emma was frying pancakes. Her hair was pulled away from her face, and as she flipped the pancake she glanced over at him.

The sparkle in her eyes dimmed, and she glanced away.

Not that he blamed her. He'd been less than diplomatic this morning, and he knew it. But her chitchat about Nana and history and how wonderful the ranch was twisted the guilt knife already lodged deep in his breast.

"I'm not sticking around long," he said. "How are you feeling today?" he asked. Yesterday, she had complained about a sore back, blaming it on her pregnancy.

"A bit stiff, but that's to be expected."

Carter put his hand on her shoulder and squeezed lightly. "You make sure you take it easy," he said.

Miranda waved her hand at him. "Don't fuss. I'm fine."

Carter gave her a gentle smile, then glanced over to catch Emma watching him. He turned away again. "I need to talk to Wade, by the way."

"He's having a shower right now." Miranda grabbed Carter by the arm and pulled him toward the table. "Sit down and eat. You're practically drooling. Emma, give this man some fresh pancakes."

"You'll really like them," Adam assured him with a grin just as Emma dropped a couple of pancakes on his plate.

"I smell pancakes," Wade called out, rubbing his hands together as he came into the kitchen. "I hope Adam didn't eat them all like he usually does."

"I don't do that," Adam complained.

Wade rubbed his head, to show him he was teasing, then flashed Carter a grin. "Glad you could join us, buddy."

In spite of Wade's smile, Carter caught an underlying note of sympathy in his voice. Since he'd been back, this was the first time Carter had stepped into the house where he used to live.

Yet another reason to get away soon. Too much subtext underneath every conversation.

"Yeah. Miranda strong-armed me into staying." He kept his tone light.

"Never mess with a pregnant woman," Miranda said. "Emma, why don't you sit down and have some breakfast? I think we have enough to eat."

"I'll throw on a few more pieces of bacon," she replied.

"Got enough of that too." Wade dropped into a chair across from Carter. "Sit down. Eat."

"Do we need more coffee?" Emma asked, not moving from her place at the stove.

"What's with the excuses? If I didn't know you better, I'd guess having the boss around was making you nervous."

To Carter's surprise, he saw a flush work its way up her neck as she sat down at the table. He doubted it was caused by nerves.

More than likely annoyance.

"I'm done." Adam licked his fingers one more time then pushed his plate away. "Can I sit on your lap, Mom?"

"Of course you can," Emma said, "But first let me wipe your hands."

Carter watched as Adam made his way around the table to Emma, unable to look away. She wiped his hands and then shifted her weight so he could sit on her lap. The domestic picture in his old kitchen teased up another memory of his nana cooking for them.

He dragged his gaze back to his foreman. "Wade, I need to talk to you. About the ranch."

"Yeah, sure. What do you need to tell me?" Wade asked, squeezing the syrup bottle over his pancakes.

Carter didn't know why he glanced over at Emma again. To his surprise, she was watching him. As if she knew what he would say.

But before Carter could speak, the phone rang. Wade reached behind him, snagging the handset off its cradle.

"Wade here," he said, tucking the phone between his shoulder and his ear as he speared a piece of bacon off the plate. Then his hand froze and his eyes widened.

"What? When?" Wade dropped his fork and gripped the phone, his fingers white. "How is he…how are they?"

He got up and strode out of the kitchen, peppering the phone with anxious questions.

Miranda shot out of her chair, leaving Emma, Adam and Carter alone in the kitchen.

Emma wrapped her arms around Adam, as if to shield him from the drama unfolding in the other room.

Carter felt his own disquiet rise at the concern in Wade's voice. Then silence, then more questions. Finally, a quiet goodbye. Wade and Miranda talking to each other. Then Wade came back into the kitchen.

"What's wrong?" Carter asked, dread sweeping over him at Wade's solemn expression. "What happened?"

Wade dropped the phone on the table and then dragged his hands over his face.

"That was Mom and Dad's pastor. My mom and dad were in a car accident. It's very serious." Wade blew out his breath, looking around the kitchen but not seeing anything. "I have to go. I have to be with them. I can't be here." He turned to Carter. "Can you stay? Until I come back? Take care of the ranch?"

Carter looked at Wade, his desire to get away from the ranch superseded by his friend's need.

"Of course I'll stay," he said.

Even as he spoke the words, he glanced over at Adam, still sitting on Emma's lap.

He had no choice. Wade needed him. But as soon as he could leave, he was gone.

Chapter Four

"Easy now. Slow it down." Carter clucked to Banjo, easing his hand down his leg and lifting his hoof. "Good job. Good horse." He patted him, then ducked under the horse's neck to do the same on the other side.

Banjo's tan hide shone from the brushing Carter gave him. He'd been working with the horse in the open paddock for the past half hour, doing some basic groundwork before he took him out. Reestablishing the relationship he'd had with this horse when he started training him three years ago.

A year before—

He cut that thought off, frustrated with the flood of memories he'd had to endure since coming back to the ranch.

His hand on Banjo's back, he glanced around at the ranch again, fighting the twist of helpless frustration. He wasn't supposed to be here. Wade was. But Wade was in the house packing up to leave, and because of that Carter was stuck here until the buyer showed up.

His eyes drifted over the familiar contours of the mountains surrounding the valley. His mother, Noelle, had moved back onto the ranch when she was expecting him and his twin brother, Garret. He never knew who his father was and, apparently, neither did his mother. At any rate, his parentage on his father's side was never discussed.

And when their mother died of cancer when Carter and Garret were ten, there was never any question of where they would live. Here. On the ranch.

Garret and Carter had grown up in the shadows of these mountains. He knew what they looked like in winter, when the cold winds surged down their snow-covered sides. In the spring when the new leaves of the aspen trees lent a counterpoint to the dark green of the spruce and fir.

He and Garret had ridden or driven down every possible game trail in and through the hills.

And when Garret went off to university to get his engineering degree, Carter had stayed behind, working on the ranch with his grandfather and eventually buying out his share.

Carter thought he'd never leave.

"How things change," he muttered, turning back to the horse. Once he was done with Banjo, he was heading out to check on the cows. In spite of his reluctance to be here, he couldn't stop a thrill of anticipation at seeing the open fields of the upper pasture. This time of the year they would be green and lush and the cattle spread out over them, calves at foot.

"He's settled down a lot the past two days."

Emma's quiet voice from the gate startled him, and as he spun around, Banjo jumped.

"Easy, boy," Carter murmured, stroking his side as he watched Emma cross the corral, leading her horses. She wore her usual blue jeans and worn cowboy boots. Today her T-shirt was blue with a rodeo logo on the front. Some remnant of her previous life. "He's got a good heart," Carter said, catching his lead rope.

"And a good nature. He's been well trained," Emma said quietly.

Carter noticed the saddles on her two horses. "Are you going out?"

"Adam and I are riding to the upper pasture."

"I'm going up there. You don't need to come along. I know where the pasture is."

Emma shot him a frown. "I'm sure you do, but I made this plan with Wade a couple of days ago. I promised Adam he could come, and he's excited to go."

"I can do this alone," he said, feeling he had to lodge one more protest. He did not want to spend any more time with the little boy than he had to.

"I'm not going to let my son down," Emma said, a hint of steel in her voice. "He's had enough disappointments for now."

Carter knew she was referring to the nonsale of the nonacreage, but it wasn't his fault the buyer probably didn't want to subdivide.

"We'll go together then," Carter said with forced nonchalance. Adam made him feel uncomfortable, but he wasn't staying behind while a stranger did the work needed on his own ranch. Though he was selling the place, he still had a stake in the ranch's well-being. And in spite of wanting to be rid of the Rocking K, a part of him wanted to see it all one last time.

Emma's horses stamped, impatient to get going.

"I'm going to water Diamond and Dusty at the river, then I'll be back," she said.

Carter looked past her and frowned again. "Where's Adam?"

"Getting some cookies for the trip. Miranda is making

up a batch to take along when they leave." Emma blew out her breath in a sigh. "I sure hope Wade's parents are okay."

She was quiet a moment, as if contemplating what Wade would have to deal with. Then she turned and led her horses to the river.

Banjo snorted and danced as Emma left with the horses.

"Easy now," he murmured, but Banjo bugled a loud whinny and Diamond stopped, tugging on his lead rope as he turned his head.

Emma tried to pull him around, but he resisted, dancing sideways. Obviously, Diamond and Banjo had bonded.

"I'll come with you," Carter said, tugging on Banjo's halter rope. "My horse could use a drink, as well."

He followed her, and both Banjo and Diamond immediately settled down.

The air, trapped in the trees edging the river, was cool. A welcome respite from the heat of the afternoon. The water burbled and splashed over the rocks, and Carter felt a sigh ease out of him. "I'd forgotten how quiet it is here," he said, glancing around as his horse drank noisily from the river.

"That's why I like coming out here to water the horses," Emma said. "Though I still can't figure out why Wade won't put a waterer in the horse corral like there is for the cows. I've seen the fittings for it coming out of the ground."

"I'm the one who won't let him," Carter said, his voice hard.

Emma shot him a puzzled glance. "Why not?"

Carter didn't want to answer the question. Obviously Wade hadn't told Emma everything. Thankfully, she sensed that he didn't want to talk about it and turned her attention back to Diamond, finger combing out the tangles in his mane.

He blew, then stamped his feet, acting like a kid getting his hair brushed.

"His hooves need trimming," Carter said, angling his chin toward Diamond's feet, eager to switch to a more mundane topic of conversation.

"I know. I haven't mastered that part of farrier work yet," Emma said. "And Wade hasn't had a chance to do it."

While he watched her, she cocked her head to one side, as if waiting for something. Then she smiled. "There's the train," Emma said.

He tilted his head, listening. Then, in the distance he heard the rumbling of the coal train, and habit made him glance at his watch. Right on time.

Dusty, her other horse, tugged at the reins, as if eager to get on with the trip, but Emma stayed where she was as the second blast of the train's horn wound its way through the valley. "I love that sound. So mournful and melancholy."

Another memory slid into Carter's mind. His grandmother stopping while she was weeding the garden to listen to the same sound. She even had the same expression on her face as Emma.

"You'll get sick enough of that noise when you hear it every day, week after week." Sylvia would complain that the train horn woke her up, but Carter had grown up with the train and seldom noticed it. He had assured her that she would eventually do the same.

"I have, and I'm not," Emma said as she led her horses back up the bank. "The routine reminds a person of where he is even if he's not aware of it. Kind of anchors you."

"Routine can deaden you too," he replied.

Emma's skeptical look at his comment as she passed him made Carter think of the miles he put on his bike and truck the past two years. The constant movement from job to job, thinking that avoiding home and familiarity would ease the pain and guilt.

Instead it was as if his sorrow was replaced by a deeper longing he couldn't fill no matter how hard he rode, how many different places he worked.

"Hey, Mom. I got cookies for our trip."

Carter's heart jumped at the sound of Adam's voice calling across the yard. He clenched his jaw and struggled once again with his reaction to Emma's little boy. He'd seen children numerous times in his travels.

He'd just never seen them riding a horse. Like Harry did. Walking around his ranch like a living reminder of what Carter didn't have anymore.

Adam sat perched on the top rail of the corral, waving a paper bag dotted with grease. "They're really good."

"Don't shake that bag too hard," Emma warned with a laugh. "You'll lose the cookies."

"And I might scare the horses," he added, lowering the bag. "Can I come down?" he asked, shifting his weight toward the edge of the fence.

"Just stay there until I get Diamond and Dusty tied up," Emma said, leading the horses past Adam.

Carter held back while Emma walked her horses through the gate, even as his gaze slipped, against his will, back to Adam, rocking back and forth on the top rail of the fence.

Carter ducked under Banjo's neck. Adam startled and pulled back.

"Mommy," he called as he flailed his arm, holding on to the bag of cookies with the other hand.

He was falling, and Emma was too far away to help.

Carter reached up and snagged him around the waist, steadying him as he slipped off the fence.

"I want my mommy," Adam said, pushing at Carter with one hand, as he tried to catch his balance. Banjo shied while Carter juggled Adam and the halter rope.

"Let me get Banjo settled," Carter said to Adam, glancing over his shoulder at his horse, who was dancing around, ears back. "Hold still. I don't want you to get hurt."

Adam stopped pushing. Carter shifted him onto his hip, caught his balance and pulled the horse's head around.

"Whoa, boy. Easy now," he murmured, walking Banjo around in a circle. His horse took a quick sidestep as he shook his head and then blew. But his ears pricked up, and Carter knew he had the horse's attention. "It's okay," he murmured, reassuring the horse.

"Will my bag of cookies scare him?" Adam said in a quiet voice, now resting one hand on Carter's shoulder.

"I don't think so," Carter said, his own heart faltering at Adam's touch. It had been two years since he held a little child. Two years since a child's arm laid on his shoulder.

Adam smelled of fresh baking and warm sun and little boy. Longing and pain rose up in Carter, and he didn't know which emotion was the strongest.

"Is everything okay?" Emma asked quietly.

"We're fine," Carter said, surprised at the tightness of his throat. When Adam saw his mother, though, he reached out for her.

Carter felt a sense of loss as Adam's weight came off his hip and the little boy's hand slipped off his shoulder. For just a moment, the emptiness had eased. For a nanosecond, his arms hadn't felt so empty.

But right behind that came the pain.

"Sorry about that," Emma said, setting Adam on the ground and then tousling his hair. "I'm sure Adam didn't mean to startle Banjo."

"No. He didn't do anything." Carter looked down at Adam, his heart beginning a heavy pounding. "I startled him, that's all. I hope Adam's okay."

Adam squinted up at him, his face scrunched up as if trying to figure Carter out. "I'm okay," he said quietly. "Thanks for helping me and for not getting mad at me."

Carter couldn't speak. How could he explain to this little boy the complications his presence created and the memories that resurfaced around him? It wasn't Adam's fault he was the same age Harry was when he died. But every time Carter saw him, the reminder of his loss plunged into his heart like a knife.

He caught Emma's enigmatic expression. As if trying to puzzle him out.

Don't bother, he wanted to tell her. *It's not worth it.*

But as their gazes caught and meshed, she gave him a careful smile, as if forgiving him his confusion.

He wasn't going to return it. He was also going to look away. But he couldn't.

Something about her called to him, and as he looked into her soft brown eyes, emotions shifted deep within him.

"Are we going now?"

Adam's voice jerked Carter back to reality and he looked away.

"That is the plan," Emma replied. "But I want to go say goodbye to Wade and Miranda first. They'll probably be gone by the time we return." She looked at Carter. "Did you want to come too?"

"I've already said goodbye," Carter said, dismissing her with a wave of his hand.

"I'll wait here with Mr. Carter." Adam flashed him a grin as if all was well between them.

"Make sure you don't eat all the cookies," Emma called back as she walked away.

"The cows are looking good," Emma said, leaning forward, her hands stacked on the saddle horn. Her eyes swept the green hills edged with fir trees, and she grinned as a half dozen calves chased each other along a fence line. Their tails were straight up and their legs stretched out. Running for no reason other than the fact that they could. Goofy creatures.

"Looks like we've got more animals on the pasture than other years," Carter said, shifting in the saddle. "I've never seen the grass so long up here before. You've done good work here."

His quiet approval warmed her heart for some silly reason. *It's because he's your boss,* she reminded herself.

"We've been doing a bit more intensive grazing this year," Emma replied, keeping her attention on the calves and not the quiet man beside her. On the ride up here he'd been quiet, watching her as if trying to figure her out.

His attention made her uncomfortable but, curiously, also created a feeling of anticipation.

"We've made the pastures smaller and moved the cows more often," she said. "Rotational grazing is more labor intensive, but I believe it lengthens the life of the pasture, which makes it possible to graze more cows on less land."

"That's a lot of fence to run."

"We use electric fencing. Run it off a solar-powered battery. That's why we come up here more often—to make sure the fence is working."

Adam's horse, Dusty, stamped, telegraphing his impatience with the lack of movement.

"Can I go up to the river?" Adam asked, cookie crumbs stuck in one corner of his mouth. "I think Dusty needs to walk a bit more, and I want to go look at that cabin." He turned to Carter. "Me and my mom found it," he explained. "It has some neat stuff in it that I want to put in the tree fort. Did you see the tree fort at the ranch, Mr. Carter?"

Carter nodded.

"I found it in the trees by the barn," Adam said, warming to his topic. "But it's not finished yet. My mom said she didn't want to do too much work on it, 'cause we might be getting the acreage. Then we can build our own fort there too. And it will be even cooler than the one we found on the ranch. And there is some really cool stuff in the cabin that I want to put in my own fort. Lanterns and stuff. Did you and your boy make that tree fort?"

Carter didn't reply, but Emma guessed, from the pensive look on Carter's face, that Adam's mention of his son hurt.

"I think Mr. Carter gets the picture," Emma said, rescuing Carter from her son's monologue. "But I don't want you going to the cabin," she warned him. "It's too far away. Just stay close, and we'll be with you in a minute." Emma wanted to check the solar panel on the fence.

"Okay, but we have to get the stuff from the cabin before someone else takes it." With that warning, Adam clucked to Dusty and, with a twist of his wrist, got him turned around.

"He seems pretty confident," Carter said, watching Adam leave.

"He's been riding horses since he was a baby," she admitted, swinging her leg over Diamond's back as she dismounted. "I used to take him up on the saddle using those buddy stirrups. He loved it. Always asked to come along when me and my dad went to check the cows. We went out a lot when I was back on the ranch." She took a breath, forcing herself to stop. Nerves, she figured. Carter's presence was a bit unsettling and she blamed her blabbering on that.

Just check the fence, she reminded herself, dropping Diamond's lead rope on the ground.

She walked over to the panel and checked the connections. All was well. Now all she needed was the tester, a small box with a digital readout that would tell her how much power was on the fence.

Carter had dismounted and was stretching his back. "It's been too long," he muttered as he took a few stiff steps.

"I'm sorry. I should have taken a break, but I didn't want to insult you by thinking you needed it," Emma said, daring a smile.

"I could have said something."

Indeed, all the way up here it had been Adam who filled the quiet with chitchat about the ranch, the horses, how the garden Miranda had put in was doing, the fair that was coming to town and, finally, the old cabin in the hills above the pasture that he wanted to get stuff from.

It wasn't lost on Emma that everything Adam said centered on the ranch. It was all he'd known since they moved here.

But Carter had remained quiet. Once in a while Emma had looked back to see if he was okay. Each time she caught him looking around, and occasionally she saw a smile. Did he miss the ranch when he was gone?

"How did you manage to teach your horse how to ground tie?" Carter asked.

Emma looked down at the lead rope she had left coiled on the ground. "Took time and patience, but Diamond figured it out eventually."

"Very impressive."

Emma bent her head over her saddlebag, wishing his compliment didn't warm her. She was supposed to be immune to him. Aloof.

But there had been a moment, when he caught Adam off the fence, that she intercepted a look of raw yearning on his face. And it hit her right in the heart, made it impossible to be indifferent to him.

She found the tester and yanked it out, but her jerky movements made the ground wire come loose. As she pulled it out, the tester's wire got twisted around the extra rope she always carried.

Everything came out in a tangle, and with a sigh she laid it on the grass by the wire fence and tugged off her gloves.

"Let me help you," Carter said, kneeling down beside her.

"It's okay. I can manage." But his nearness made her hands clumsy and unresponsive, leading to a worse mess.

"So have you made any plans for after the sale of the ranch?" she asked, latching onto the one subject guaranteed to maintain a distance between them.

"No solid plans. I'll see what happens when the time comes, same as I have for a while now." He pulled the box of the tester free from the tangle and unplugged the wire coming from it.

In that moment their hands brushed, and Emma jerked hers back.

This netted her a puzzled look from Carter. This was silly. Why was she so tense around him?

She leaned back on her heels, her hands still holding

the rope she had just freed. "So you've just been moving from place to place?"

"Pretty much. I just try to find a job where they provide a place to live—either a camp job or a ranch job." Carter shot her a quick glance as he shoved the grounding portion of the tester into the grass.

Emma's hands slowed as she looked past Carter to the land flowing away from them, the mountains with their jagged lines of purple against the sky.

"I can't imagine being away from here."

Carter's eyes followed the direction of her gaze, and she saw his features relax. In that moment, she caught a sense of longing in his eyes.

"I missed it, in some ways." A melancholy smile drifted across his lips. "I grew up here, after all. As did my mother, my grandfather and his father."

"Nana Beck told me a bit of the history of the place," Emma said. "But when she talked about the necklace, that was the first I'd heard about August and Kamiskahk."

Carter released a light laugh. "My cousins Hailey, Shannon and Naomi liked that story more than me and Garret did when we were kids."

"Why?"

"August gave up searching for gold for the sake of a mere girl. Garret and I both said we wouldn't have done that. In fact, Garret and I even went up into the mountains once, looking for the same gold, armed with shovels and bags to carry all the gold we were going to find." Carter toyed with the contacts for the fence tester, squinting up at the mountain above them. "Of course, at age ten, girls weren't a real priority."

Emma laughed, trying to imagine two young boys hiking up the mountain, shovels over their shoulders.

"I don't imagine you found any," she said.

"Nope. Naomi was very disappointed with us when we came back empty-handed. She had imagined all the pretty things she was going to make with the gold we found. Hailey just figured we could sell it and get rich." He laughed again, and in that moment, Emma caught a glimpse of what Carter must have been like before his loss. She saw a man connected to a place and a family that he cared for.

And she also felt a twinge of jealousy at the connections he had. Cousins. Grandparents. A place that had history and continuity.

"Shannon didn't have any plans for the gold?"

"Shannon's always been the most practical of us all. She knew me and Garret would come back empty-handed. So no, she didn't have any plans." He laughed, then placed the contacts on the electric fence to test the power. "And speaking of plans, what do you plan to do, once the ranch is sold?" he asked.

Emma reluctantly returned to the present, wondering why he cared about her plans. "I guess I'll have to decide once that happens." She still planned on going into town on Thursday to look for a job and, hopefully, a place where she could board her horses.

Carter looked up at her, his eyes holding hers. "Again, I'm sorry about how this is all coming down for you."

She didn't want his sympathy, but at the same time, it still created a faint connection. She felt sorry for him, after all, and for even bigger things than the loss of a job.

"Well, that's life." She shrugged and glanced down at the meter in his hand. "How's the reading on the fence?"

Carter glanced down at the readout. "Looks good," he said. Then he rolled the wire back around the tester. "I could talk to the buyer. See if maybe you could work for him. I'm not sure Wade wants to stay on, but it might be an option for you."

"I want more than just a job out of the ranch. I'm looking for a place to settle down. A home. So Adam and I will be moving on. Again." Why did she tack that "again" on? It sounded whiny, and if there's one thing Emma knew, "whiny" turned men away faster than tears. She learned that quick enough from Adam's father and from Karl.

She pushed the bitter memories aside. That was in the past. She had to focus on the future.

"But where would you go?" Carter asked.

"I guess that's nothing you need to concern yourself with," she said, catching Diamond's rope and vaulting back into the saddle.

As soon as she got Diamond turned around, she regretted her snappy reply. His question was a way of making conversation, but it dragged out concerns and worries Emma struggled to keep suppressed.

Yet, as she headed down the trail to where Adam had gone, she wished she'd been more diplomatic.

She also wished she knew what it was about Carter that made her feel extra edgy around him.

Chapter Five

Carter pulled up on Banjo's bridle and blew out a sigh of relief. Thankfully, he had made it to the yard before Emma and Adam. Adam wanted to stop a ways back to check out some mushrooms growing along the river so Carter, seeing a way to salvage his pride, said he would meet them at the corral.

Without them as witnesses, he allowed himself to groan as he dismounted, muscles he hadn't used in years protesting every movement.

Banjo turned his head as if to ask Carter what the problem was.

"It's been too long," he muttered to Banjo, absently rubbing the horse's neck. "That kid is in better shape than I am."

He put his hands in the small of his back and stretched, then rotated his shoulders. He was tender in places he knew he would feel for the next few days. It would take a bit more riding before he could be as fluid in the saddle as Emma.

He shot a worried glance over his shoulder, but thankfully she wasn't coming up the riverbank yet.

He took a few halting steps, pain shooting up his legs,

and then sighed again as he unwound Banjo's halter rope from the saddle horn. He led the horse to the corral by the tack shed, every step causing pain in one muscle or the other. He would be a hurtin' unit tomorrow.

He undid the cinch and unsaddled Banjo. By the time he got the bridle off, his horse whinnied and turned his head, signaling Emma and Adam's approach.

"Look at the cool mushroom I found, Mr. Carter. There was a whole bunch."

Carter glanced over at Adam who held up a creamy mushroom with an undulating cap. "Chanterelles are good eating," he said quietly. "And they are hard to find around here."

"Mom said she was going to cook them. With our supper."

Supper. The thought made his stomach growl. All he'd had to eat since breakfast was a couple of cookies and a granola bar that Emma had shared with him, insisting that she didn't mind.

Nana Beck had gone with Shannon to town for a doctor's appointment and to look at potential places to live, so he was on his own for dinner. Looked as if cold cereal was on the menu.

Emma dismounted in one graceful motion and then helped Adam out of the saddle. With quick, efficient movements that made Carter both envious and a bit humiliated, she tugged the cinches loose on both horses and pulled the saddles off one at a time.

He felt like an unchivalrous heel, but manhandling his own saddle onto the saddle tree in the tack shed was all he could manage.

"A bit stiff?" she asked, a smile hovering at one corner of her mouth as she dropped the saddles on their respective trees.

He was about to protest but realized it was futile.

"Oh, yeah." He dropped the saddle blanket on an empty rack and groaned again.

"Make sure you do some stretches before you go to bed tonight. A brisk walk helps too." Emma looped the cinch ropes over the horns of the saddles. "I'm sorry the ride was so long. I forgot that you hadn't ridden in a while."

Carter rubbed the tops of his legs and eased out a sigh. "Over a year ago."

"You didn't have to come," she said quietly, snagging the curry comb and brushes off a shelf.

"Until the ranch changes ownership, it's still my responsibility. But now all I want to do is go lie down in my cabin and try to work up the energy to think about dinner."

Emma picked a clump of horsehair out of the brush, avoiding his gaze. "About that… Miranda made a casserole for us. I'll go heat it up, and if you want we can eat it together in the house. I was thinking of frying up the mushrooms to go with it," she added, "if that extra incentive will change your mind."

He looked over at her and caught a dimple forming in a cheek that held a smudge of dirt. She pushed her hair back from her face, and as she held his gaze her soft brown eyes held a gentle light of understanding.

He felt a light thrum of awareness, and the thought of eating with her created a sense of anticipation. But it also meant spending time with Adam.

"Just come," she said, her voice quiet, as if she understood his reluctance. "It's only food."

She gave him a gentle smile, and as their eyes met he dismissed his other concerns. "Sounds like a plan. Thanks." Then he held out his hand for the brushes. "Give those to me. I'll finish up with the horses."

"I can do them."

He waved his hand in a "gimme" gesture. "I'm just stiff. The work will do me good."

With a light laugh, she relinquished the brushes. "Okay. Adam and I will be in the house. Give me about half an hour." Then she spun around and strode out of the shed.

In the quiet she left in her wake, second thoughts followed. Could he really sit down in his old house and have dinner with Emma and Adam? Could he really act as if everything was okay?

Carter shook his questions aside. It was time, he figured. If he was selling this ranch, it was time to lay some memories to rest, as well. Then he could walk away from this place with no second thoughts. No regrets.

Emma set the third plate on the table, wondering for the umpteenth time what got into her when she invited Carter for dinner.

Mistake. Mistake.

The words had resonated through her head with each tick of the clock on the timer counting down when the casserole would be ready.

The mushrooms were sautéing in the pan, and Adam lay sprawled on the floor behind the table. She couldn't see what he was doing, but he was humming to himself, happy.

"Today was a good day, wasn't it, buddy?" she asked.

"Yup."

"Did you enjoy the riding?"

"Yup."

"What was the best part of the day?" Open-ended questions, she reminded herself.

"The mushrooms."

"Why were they the best?"

"Because."

Emma turned off the heat under the pan and walked around the table to where Adam lay putting together a puzzle. She crouched down and grinned at him.

"Are you playing a game with me?"

He looked up at her and flashed a grin. "Yup."

She rubbed the top of his head. "I wondered what you were up to. For a minute there you sounded like Mr. Carter."

"He doesn't like to talk, does he?" Adam asked, reaching for another piece. Emma thought of the memories Carter had shared with her. He was more reserved around Adam, though.

"Mr. Carter has a lot on his mind. That's why he's so quiet," she said. "He's not like your mommy, who likes to fill the empty spaces in conversation with lots and lots of words." She picked up a puzzle piece and fitted it in an empty space, and then she pushed herself to her feet and turned around.

Carter Beck stood in the doorway, a light frown creasing his forehead, and she wondered if he had heard what she and Adam were talking about.

"Supper is ready," she said, glancing nervously at the timer, deciding to pretend he hadn't.

"Smells good in here," Carter said, taking a step farther into the kitchen. He angled his head, as if looking at Adam on the floor behind the table.

Adam got up and slipped into the chair he usually sat at. He pointed at the place setting across from him. "That's where you're supposed to sit, Mr. Carter."

Carter gave him a quick nod but glanced over at Emma. "Is there anything I can do?"

"I think I've got it under control. If you want to contribute, you can put these on the table." She handed him the bowl holding the sautéed mushrooms, then gave him a careful smile, which he returned.

She felt her cheeks flush and blamed it on the heat in the kitchen as she pulled open the oven door. The casserole bubbled, and steam slipped out from the lid.

It went on the table as well, and then there was nothing left to do but sit down.

Carter waited until she sat down. Just a small gesture, but it touched her. Whenever Karl came over to eat, he would serve himself even before she and her father sat down.

When they were all seated, there was a moment of quiet. Then, to her surprise, Adam reached across the table, one hand outstretched to Emma, the other to Carter.

Carter glanced from his hand to Emma, as if asking her what to do.

"We usually pray before our meals," she gently suggested, taking Adam's hand.

"And we hold hands," Adam added.

Carter gave a tight nod, then reached across the table and caught Adam's hand. But Adam's little gesture had put her in an uncomfortable position.

"Mom, you have to hold Mr. Carter's hand," Adam said, giving her hand a squeeze. "That's the way we always did it at Grandpa's."

"Of course," she said with a light laugh. As she put her hand in Carter's, she felt ridiculously aware of the size of his hand and the callouses on his palms.

Then she bowed her head, trying to focus her thoughts on God and not on the rough hand that held her own.

"Thank You, Lord, for this food," she prayed, letting herself be drawn into God's presence. "Thank You for this day and the wonderful time we had outside in Your creation. Be with Miranda and Wade as they travel, and be with Wade's parents. Be with Nana Beck as she looks for a place in town. Help her to be better. Bless this food unto our bodies and help us to be thankful for all You give us and help us to love You. Amen."

She kept her head bowed for a moment longer, then slipped her hands out of Adam's and Carter's.

"So, I hope you like chicken casserole," she said with false brightness as she got up to serve the food. "Miranda's a great cook and does a fantastic job on this casserole. I've had it a bunch of times, so I'm sure you'll like it. I'm pretty sure it's hot enough. It was bubbling when I took it out of the stove, I mean, oven."

"Why are you talking so much, Mom?" Adam asked, handing Emma his plate.

Because she was nervous. Because when they were outside, there was space and distance between her and Carter and Adam.

Now they were all together in this small kitchen, and she felt as if there wasn't enough room or enough air.

But obviously she kept all this to herself while she shot her son a warning look. He frowned and opened his mouth as if to add more words of wisdom to the conversation.

"Do you want some salad?" she asked him, cutting him off.

He wrinkled his nose, thankfully distracted. "I don't like salad." He pulled his plate back, just to make sure she didn't sneak some on while he wasn't looking.

Emma held her hand out for Carter's plate, avoiding his gaze, excessively conscious of his presence and wishing for a moment she hadn't invited him. But what else could she have done? Let him sit in a cabin all by himself?

"Sure smells good," Carter said, taking his plate from Emma.

He filled the rest of his plate with salad and waited until she'd served herself to start eating. Again, a small courtesy, but it gave her a glimpse of how he treated women. He seemed at ease, which made Emma relax a bit. She was being silly. They had spent most of the day together. Why was she so conscious of him now?

Because this was such a family moment, she thought, sprinkling salt over her food. A man, a woman and a child sharing a meal together.

Her heart quavered as she set the salt shaker down. How often had she pictured herself, Karl and Adam sitting around their own kitchen table sharing a meal, just the three of them?

She stabbed her salad, glancing over at Carter, determined to act naturally. "How are the mushrooms?"

"Really good," he said, giving her a cautious smile.

"I think they taste like elastics," Adam said.

Emma laughed, and to her surprise, a smile twitched at the corner of Carter's mouth.

"Did you live here when you were little?" Adam asked Carter, stabbing a noodle from the casserole and holding it up for inspection.

Carter's only reply was a quick nod.

"Were you borned here?" Adam continued, undaunted by Carter's seeming reticence.

"Yes. I was."

"On the ranch? Here?" Adam poked his finger down at the floor.

"Actually, yeah."

"Was your boy borned here?"

"Yes." His reply was quiet, and Emma sensed Adam wasn't going to get much more out of Carter.

"Did your wife choose home birth?" she asked, trying to maintain a semblance of conversation.

"Not on purpose." Carter gave her a quick smile but turned his attention back to his food.

"I was borned in a hospital," Adam offered. He glanced at Emma. "Why wasn't I borned in a house?"

"Because your mother is a scaredy-cat and liked to have doctors and medication handy," she said, giving her son a wink so he would know she was kidding. A bit.

"You're not a scaredy-cat," Adam said, mumbling around a mouthful of pasta. He turned back to Carter, determined to engage the man one way or the other. "My mommy and I were riding and we met a bear and my mommy didn't get scared or anything. The horses got scared but my mommy told me to hang on and she made the horses get quiet again. Then the bear was gone. So my mommy is not a scaredy-cat."

This caught Carter's attention. "Really? Where was that?"

Emma glanced at Adam, half hoping he would handle the question for her, but Carter was looking at her and Adam was frowning at his plate.

"Adam and I went on a short trip to the Ya Ha Tinda, past Sundre," she said, glad to have fixed on a neutral topic. "We were up in the alpine, and a grizzly bear happened to wander across the trail."

"Really? Been a while since I've seen a grizzly. You must have been pretty tense."

"I was, but I had Adam to think about, and I couldn't afford to get too scared."

"I imagine the horses freaked."

"They spun around and were heading back down the trail, but I had to get them turned around so I could see what was happening. Thankfully, Adam hung on, and

I got things sorted out. By the time I did, the bear was gone."

"Wow. That's some horsemanship." Carter sounded impressed and Emma couldn't help a flicker of pride.

She shot him a quick glance, surprised to see him looking at her. Their eyes met, held, and a tiny spark of awareness flashed between them.

Don't go there, Emma thought. *This is temporary.*

"My mommy is really brave," Adam put in, breaking the moment. "Was Harry's mommy brave?"

Carter stiffened as Adam spoke. He blinked and then looked down at his half-finished casserole. He poked some of the noodles around then dropped his knife and fork on the plate with a clatter. "You know, this was great. But I think I'm full." He shoved his chair back, the legs screeching on the worn linoleum, and strode to the counter, depositing his plate on it. "Thanks for dinner," he said absently, and then he grabbed his hat off the end of the counter and left.

"Is Mr. Carter mad?" Adam asked, lowering his hands to his lap, his lip quivering. "Did I make him mad?"

Emma suspected that he had. And she also suspected that Carter's anger was born out of loss. But the sorrow lacing her son's voice cut her to the core.

She reached over and stroked her son's hand then took it in hers. "Mr. Carter is a very sad man. And I think that you remind him of his little boy, Harry."

This made Adam smile. "I do?" He swiped the back of his hand across his nose.

"Yes, you do. Maybe you shouldn't talk about Harry so much. Because we don't want to make Mr. Carter sad again, okay?"

Adam seemed to consider this, then nodded. "Okay."

"Now finish up your casserole and I'll let you watch *The Wind in the Willows* while I'm cleaning up."

This was all the incentive he needed. Five minutes later, his plate was licked clean, his hands washed and he lay curled up in a chair in front of Wade and Miranda's television, entertained by the adventures of Mole, Ratty and Toad.

Emma made quick work of the dishes. There was half of the casserole left, which they could have for dinner tomorrow. As she covered it up and put it in the refrigerator, she wondered whether she would repeat dinner with Carter.

Obviously Carter felt uncomfortable around Adam, and while she understood why, she didn't know how to deal with this every day. It wasn't fair to Adam, and it was too hard on her.

She lowered the dishes into the soapy water, her mind and heart at war. She needed this job, but was it worth putting Adam through all this tension? She could try to keep Adam away from Carter but how to do that and help on the ranch at the same time? Besides, once the ranch was sold, she was on her way anyhow. Why postpone the decision?

But then Carter would be left here alone. And that thought disturbed her on another level.

Dear Lord, she prayed as she scrubbed the dishes, *help me around this little mess.*

Twenty minutes later she cleaned up the last dish. She was about to leave for the living room when the phone rang.

"Is this Miranda?" a woman's voice asked when she picked up.

"No. I'm sorry, Miranda and Wade will be gone for a while. This is Emma Minton."

"The girl who works on the ranch?"

"That's right." Emma frowned. "Can I ask who is calling?"

"I'm sorry. It's Kim Groot. Miranda was telling me about you the last time I called. I'm…I'm Harry's grandmother."

Chapter Six

"You are Carter's mother-in-law?" Emma clutched the handset, wishing Carter could have taken this call. This wasn't her place. She shouldn't be the one talking to this woman.

"I've been staying in touch with Miranda, hoping to connect with Carter. She, uh, well, she called me to tell me…that Carter was back." In the pause following this, Emma heard a light sniff, followed by a wavering intake of breath. "I'm so sorry. It's just…I haven't talked to Carter since Harry's funeral. Is he…is he there?"

"I'm sorry, no." Emma leaned against the wall, clutching the handset. She felt a surge of pity for this woman who had lost so much. A daughter, a grandson and, it seemed, Carter, as well. "He's staying in one of the cabins. I can take your number and get him to call you."

A sigh followed this. "You can try. My husband and I have been trying to call him on his cell phone, but he doesn't answer."

Emma frowned, puzzled as to why Carter was avoiding Harry's grandparents. Surely he would want to talk to them?

She walked to the counter and pulled a pen and paper

out of a drawer. "Give me your number and I'll mention it to him."

"I think he knows it, but I'll give you the information anyway."

Emma tucked the handset between her shoulder and ear while she scribbled down the number. "Okay. I think I've got it."

"Thanks so much," Kim said. "When you see Carter, could you please tell him that we miss him? And that we love him."

"I'll do that," she said.

She said goodbye, then wrote a note to Carter asking him to please call Kim Groot. She put Kim's number under that and tacked it to the bulletin board under the piece of paper with the number of Wade's parents' home.

She hesitated, wondering if she should call Wade and find out what was happening.

Later, she told herself. First she had other things to deal with. She went to the living room. The television was still on, but Adam lay curled up on the couch, fast asleep.

She knelt down beside him and stroked his hair away from his face, her heart growing soft at the sight of his relaxed features, his rosy cheeks. The utter innocence of her son asleep.

And his utter vulnerability.

As she fingered some hair away from his face, she thought again of the various hurts and disappointments he'd already had to deal with in his life. Karl. Her father's death. Having to leave the ranch.

And now the stress of Carter's reaction to him.

Again she reminded herself of the vow she made after Karl had left her and Adam. How she would always put Adam's needs and care first. How his well-being was her first priority.

And if being on the ranch was causing him problems, she had to make a decision.

She wrapped an afghan around him, then bent over and fitted her arms under his knees and around his shoulders. As she went to lift him, she stumbled.

When did he get so heavy? She still thought of him as her little boy, but he wasn't so little anymore. As she shifted him in her arms, she felt a stirring of nostalgia. She felt as if only a year had passed since she could cradle him close to her chest. Now his legs and head dangled over her arms. One day he would be taller than she.

Shouldering the door open, she quashed that thought, far too aware of the responsibilities he created now. Bad enough that he would be starting school soon. She didn't need to project her worries too far in the future.

She stepped outside into the cool of the evening, his weight slowing her steps. His head lolled against her chest, and she looked down at him. He was so precious to her. He was all she had.

And it was that realization that steeled her for what she had to do next.

Once in the cabin, she managed to get his pajamas on without waking him too much. Then, when he was tucked in his bed, the blanket pulled up around his rosy cheeks, she sat a moment, watching him. He was her responsibility, and she was the only one who could protect him.

When his breathing was deep and heavy, she pushed herself to her feet, fear thrumming through her.

Please, Lord, she prayed as she stepped out of the cabin. *Please let me make the right decision. Help me to trust You and to trust that You will help me take care of my boy.*

Dusk was gathering as she walked across the yard. Golden light glowed from the windows of Carter's cabin.

She sent up another quick prayer as she walked up the steps and knocked on the door.

Carter opened the door, frowning at her. "Is everything okay?" The light of the cabin backlit him, throwing his features in shadow. He cut an imposing figure, and for a split second she wanted to change her mind. "Is Adam—"

"Adam is sleeping," she said, her hands clasped in front of her, determined to follow through on this. "Can I...can I talk to you?"

Carter stepped aside, opening the door farther. "Sure. Of course. Come in."

Emma would have preferred to talk to him outside. He still made her uncomfortable, but saying no looked rude. So she nodded and stepped inside.

"Can I get you anything," he asked as he pulled an old chair out for her. "Tea? Coffee?"

"Actually, I'm fine," she said, holding up one hand. "I'm not staying that long."

Carter shrugged then pulled out an old armchair from beside the stove for her to sit on. When Carter dropped to the edge of the bed, she sat down, as well.

"So what can I do for you?" He rested his elbows on his knees, clasping his hands as he leaned forward. His blue eyes met hers, and Emma couldn't stop a glimmer of attraction as a smile tipped up one corner of his mouth.

He seemed more relaxed than he had been around Adam, which stiffened her resolve. "I need to talk to you about Adam," she said, getting directly to the point.

Carter frowned. "Sure. What about him?"

She rubbed her hands on her thighs, trying to formulate what she wanted to say. "You seem uncomfortable around him."

Carter straightened, his gaze dropping to his hands. "What do you mean?"

"You know what I mean," Emma said, lowering her voice. Trying to sound nonconfrontational. Understanding. "It wasn't as obvious when we were out checking the cows in the pasture, but it was there, as well. Supper time was when it really came to a head."

Carter's frown deepened, but he said nothing.

"In fact, he asked me why you were angry with him."

Carter pushed himself off his bed, turning away from her. "I'm not angry with him. I…" His sentence trailed off as he tunneled his hand through his hair.

"I know you're not angry with him, but that's how he's reading your actions. And I'm guessing it was because this evening was uncomfortable for you. I'm sorry that we invited you. I mean, not sorry in the sense that I regret it for my sake…" She caught herself, stumbling along through this potential conversational minefield while Carter stood with his back to her, his hands now planted on his hips. "I…I mean for your sake. I'm sorry for your sake. It must have been difficult to see Adam sitting in the kitchen. And I'm guessing it was a stark reminder of…of your son."

She stopped there, waiting for a reaction from him.

Carter grabbed the back of his neck, still turned away from her. Still silent, but his resistance was a tangible force swirling around the cabin.

She drew in a long breath, forcing herself to continue. She had to get this out of the way.

"I know from talking to Wade and your grandmother that you haven't been back here since the accident," she said, her heart pushing heavily against her chest. "So you haven't had a chance to get used to the idea he isn't here anymore. And I'm sure seeing Adam…seeing me in that kitchen was difficult." She closed her eyes and sucked in a deep breath, desperately sending up scattered prayers.

She was doing this all wrong. She was only making this worse for him.

Carter turned around, holding her gaze. "Is this why you came? To tell me that you understand what I'm going through?" His words lay heavy between them.

"Partly," she said, licking her lips, her hands like ice. "But…I had another reason."

"Like telling me how sorry you feel for me? Telling me how sad it is that I lost my son and that I'll get over it?"

Oh, Lord, what have I started?

She waited, letting the silence ease away the echoes of his voice. Then she took another breath. "I had no intention of trying to give you advice or to minimize what you've gone through. I'm only trying to tell what I'm seeing from my side of the situation and how it's—"

"Situation? What situation?"

Emma squeezed her hands into fists, praying for patience. Sure, he was a grieving father, and, sure, he lost a lot. But she had a problem to solve, and if no solution was in sight she had to make a major decision.

"While I respect your sorrow and grief, it's causing a problem for my son," Emma said, looking down at her hands, her fingers braided together on her lap. "As badly as I feel for you, my…my situation is that Adam and his well-being are my first priority. And right now, he's afraid of you. And if that doesn't change, I can't continue to work under these circumstances."

Silence followed this formal pronouncement, and Carter turned around then slowly dropped onto the bed. He grabbed his head with his hands, his fingers clenching in his hair.

"I know. I'm sorry."

His admission surprised her. Given his frustration, she thought he would simply tell her, fine. Leave.

He released his breath, then looked up at her.

"I know I'm uncomfortable around Adam. And you're right. He does remind me of…of my son." Carter looked away and pulled in another shaky breath. "And it does hurt.

"But right now, to keep the ranch going, I need you to stay. You know how things work here. I haven't been around enough to know your and Wade's system." He lifted his shoulders in a deep sigh. "I don't know how my own ranch runs. And until the buyer comes or Wade returns, I need your help."

Though she knew he referred to the ranch, on another level it felt good to know that Carter needed her.

"And I'm sorry about Adam," Carter continued. "He's a good kid. I like him…" Carter's voice faded away and his lips curved in a wistful smile. "You're doing a good job with him."

Emma waited, letting the moment settle, giving him space to deal with his own pain.

Then he looked up at her, his eyes locking on to hers. "If I promise to try to deal with all of this, will you stay?" Carter asked.

Emma held his gaze and heard the entreaty in his voice. She struggled to balance the needs of her son with what this handsome, appealing man was asking of her.

Should she?

Emma caught her lower lip between her teeth, trying to weigh her reactions, her feelings. Part of her wanted to jump up, grab Adam and leave.

Yet the practical part of her realized that she had no other place to go. And no other real options. Yet.

"Okay," she said quietly. "If you can deal with Adam's presence, then I'll stay."

"Good. Thanks." He gave her a careful smile, his eyes still holding hers.

Emma couldn't look away. It seemed as if time slowed while awareness fluttered between them. A hesitant shift in the atmosphere that both enticed and frightened her.

She made herself look away. Made herself break the moment.

"Sylvia's mother called."

The words came out more blunt than she had hoped. But they definitely created the switch in the mood she needed.

Carter straightened and blinked, as if pulling himself from another place. "When?"

"Earlier tonight. She didn't know Miranda and Wade were gone."

"What did she want?"

The stiffness of his features made her realize her blunt pronouncement had served its purpose. And yet, the lonely part of her yearned foolishly for that small moment of closeness they shared only seconds ago.

"She wants to talk to you."

Carter got to his feet and walked to the door, then back to the bed and then to the stove. "What about?"

You passed the message on. You're done. This isn't your problem. This isn't your place. Just leave, already.

But when she saw his face, the pain and sorrow that had returned, she knew she couldn't drop Sylvia's mother into the conversation and then leave, in spite of her need to protect herself and Adam.

"I think she misses you," she said quietly.

"Why would she?"

Emma thought of her own lack of connections. Her father gone. Her grandparents dead. One aunt who lived in a retirement village in Florida. No uncles. Karl, a man she had hoped to spend her life with, gone. The paucity of relationships made her, for a moment, envy Carter in spite of his loss.

"You are the only connection they have to their daughter and grandson." She pressed on, not sure why this had become so important to her, but she wanted him to understand what he kept himself from. "I lost my mother when I was young. I used to love it when my father would tell me stories about her. They became my way of connecting with her. Of feeling as if the hole her absence left wasn't as big. I think she wants to talk to you about Harry. To share stories."

Carter shook his head, as if he couldn't believe her. "A person has to move on. Living in the past serves no purpose. Waste of time. Waste of emotions." Beneath his words, Emma heard a note of yearning that called to her.

And the sorrow on his face eased past the barriers she'd been trying to erect to keep him at a distance.

She leaned forward, trying to catch his eye. "Have you talked to your in-laws at all?"

Carter emitted a short laugh. "I left right after the funeral. I couldn't get away from here fast enough. Why does this matter to you?"

She held his gaze and gave him a melancholy smile. "I've also gotten to know your family a bit working here on the ranch. They also lost something when Sylvia then Harry died. And they lost something when you left too. They lost your stories."

"Look, all I want is some peace in my life. And to get away from all the emotions and the crying and the pain. Now that my grandmother is moving off the ranch, I can put this part of my life behind me. Get some peace."

"And do you have peace now?"

Carter opened his mouth as if to speak, but then he

shook his head. "I don't know. And talking about my son isn't going to get me what I want."

"But the longer you wait to talk about your son..." She hesitated, realizing in a moment of blinding clarity that he never mentioned Harry's name aloud. She wondered if anyone ever did in front of him, other than Adam.

She plunged ahead, "The longer you wait to talk about Harry, the harder it's going to be. It will hurt, but I think you need to get through this stage."

He said nothing to that, and Emma figured she had said enough, as well. And had spent enough time here. She had her own problems to deal with, and she had to be careful not to get pulled too deeply into Carter's.

He had to make his own decisions, and his problems weren't hers. Once the buyer came here, she would be gone and Carter would be out of her life.

She got up to leave, but the sight of this strong, silent man, sitting alone on the bed, his face in his hands, tugged at her heart.

She touched his shoulder, hoping to give him some connection. Some small comfort.

He eased out a sigh then, to her surprise, his hand came up and covered hers. The warmth of his large hand eased into the closed-off portion of her heart.

She waited a few heartbeats, reminding herself what she had wanted to say.

"You say you can't talk to your family about Harry, but you might want to think about talking to God," she said quietly.

He lowered his hand, breaking the connection, creating a momentary sense of loss. "Do you think that will help?" He looked up at her, the broken longing in his gaze calling to her. "I feel like I'm all alone in this."

Emma slipped her hands in her pockets and drew in a breath. "God never lets us go, Carter."

"How can you say that with such conviction?" The faint note of uncertainty in his voice gave her hope.

"I lost a father. I lost a fiancé. I lost hopes and dreams." *And I'm in the process of shelving a few more,* she thought.

"But the one constant in my life," she continued, "Has been my need to depend on God. To connect with Him."

Carter blinked then looked away, shoving his hand through his thick hair. "I don't know if I can start again. I've been away so long."

"God is faithful." Emma sensed his receptiveness to what she was saying. "And He wants us to be in a relationship with Him." She hesitated, wondering if she had overstepped the boundaries, but her concern for him outweighed her reticence. "It's Sunday tomorrow. Why don't you come to church? Reconnect with the people that care about you. Bring your questions to God and see if you can find a bit of the peace you've been trying to find."

Silence followed that, but Carter didn't shrug off her suggestion. Nor did he mock her declaration.

She waited a moment, then realizing she had said more than enough, went back to her cabin.

Half an hour later the sound of his motorbike roared into the night, growing quieter as he drove away. As if he was outrunning his own pain and sorrow.

Chapter Seven

Carter parked his motorbike, pulled his helmet off his head and hung it on the handlebars. He finger combed his hair and checked it in the rearview mirror of his bike. Not great, but it would have to do.

He adjusted his jacket then looked across the parking lot to the church building, gleaming in the morning sunlight.

He hesitated, examining again his reasons for being here. Nana would love it. It was what the Beck family did every Sunday. Tradition.

But even as he examined his motive, he knew something else had drawn him here this morning. The quiet comment Emma had made last night had chipped away at his resistance to God. He had gone out on a long ride last night, but he couldn't quiet the angry questions he had thrown toward heaven after Harry's death.

Emma's challenge to take those questions to the source stuck with him. So he decided to come to church this morning and face God directly. If nothing came of it, he could say he tried. And maybe, just maybe, he could find his elusive peace as Emma had said.

As he stepped through the doors, a burst of noise

greeted him. Groups of people gathered in the foyer of the church, talking and laughing. Children ran among the adults, playing a rambunctious game of hide-and-seek. The door behind him opened again, and two young girls ran past him to join in the game.

He recognized a number of people. One woman close to him turned. Carter could tell the moment she recognized him. Her eyes widened, her hand fluttered to her chin and sympathy flooded her features.

Carter only gave her a tight smile, then quickly worked his way through the crowd to the sanctuary. He wasn't ready to face sympathy. Not yet.

A quick scan of the half-full pews helped him spot his grandmother and cousin. He hurried down the aisle. He slipped past a purse lying at the end of the pew and dropped onto the empty space beside his grandmother, enjoying Nana's surprised reaction.

"Carter, how wonderful to see you here." She slipped her arm through his. As she pulled him close, he caught the faintest scent of roses and hairspray, two smells he always associated with Nana and Sunday. "This makes me so happy." She drew back, her contented smile erasing all the second thoughts that had dogged him all the way here. If Nana was happy, he was happy.

Shannon leaned past Nana and gave him a quick smile and a nod of approval, her auburn, curly hair bouncing as she did. Carter was surprised to see her here. Only a month ago he knew she'd been working on decorations for the church for her wedding. When her fiancé called it off and left town, he'd been told that Shannon had stayed away from church too.

But now she was here too, and he suspected it was for the same reason he was. To make Nana Beck happy.

Though, as he settled into the bench beside Nana, he

knew, beneath the desire to please his grandmother lay a deeper reason.

"You didn't bring your Bible?" Nana asked, frowning at his empty hands.

"Uh, no...I came on my motorbike."

"They have Bibles in the back." A gentle smile accompanied her suggestion, but Carter easily read the subtext.

"Save my place," he said with a wink as he got up. He walked past people coming in, giving vague smiles and replies to those who greeted him by name.

"Carter. You old pirate." A deep voice boomed across the foyer. Carter almost winced then turned to face Matt Thomas, an old school friend.

The last time Carter saw Matt, he was thinner and had hair. Now his shaved head gleamed under the bright lights of the church entrance and a goatee covered his double chin. A leather jacket blazer and black jeans strained against the extra weight across his waist. "Wow, it's been a coon's age since you've been here," Matt said, slapping Carter on the shoulder. "I heard you were back to see your grandma. How is the old matriarch? Heard she had a heart attack?"

"She's doing much better. She's here now," Carter said then gave his old friend a grin. "So what's with the biker look?"

Matt ran his hand over his shiny head. "Not all of us are blessed with shag carpeting for hair. You trying to pull a Sampson?"

"Nope. Just haven't had time for a cut."

"Next free day you have you come around to Laurie's shop. She'll have you trimmed, gelled and moussed quicker'n you can say *hair product*. Then you and me can head over to the Royal for burgers and the best fries in

Hartley Creek." Matt slapped Carter on the back. "Like old times."

"That'd be good." Carter grabbed a Bible off the rack and raised it toward Matt. "Sounds like a date."

He was about to leave, thankful for the lighthearted banter he had shared with Matt.

Then Matt put his hand on his shoulder, his eyes grew moist and Carter inwardly braced himself.

And here it comes.

"Buddy, I'm so sorry about what happened to you," Matt said, moving closer as people flowed past them. "Sorry about Harry. I never had a chance to talk to you. You disappeared right after the funeral."

Carter shifted the Bible from hand to hand. "It's been a while. Two years now."

Matt squeezed a little harder. "I know, but it still must be hard. That's something you don't get over real quick. I want you to know that me and Laurie, well, we been praying for you."

Carter stopped, then looked up at his friend, surprised at how touched he was by the comment. He was moved to know that someone other than his grandmother kept his name before God.

He gave Matt a careful smile. "Thanks for that," he said.

An awkward pause followed and Carter took a step away, poking his thumb over his shoulder. "Gotta get back to my grandmother. Told her I'd be right back."

Matt nodded, but as Carter returned to the pew, he realized a couple of things. Talking to Matt hadn't been as hard as he'd thought.

And Emma was right about her comment about community. He was looking forward to catching up with Matt, an old friend who knew him before his life fell apart.

The building had filled while he was gone, and he had to scan the now-full pews to find his grandmother.

He found her, but as he was about to step into the bench, he paused.

Emma sat at one end, rooting through the purse parked there previously. Adam sat beside her, leaning over to see what she was digging around for.

She wore a long pink sweater over a cream-colored tank top and a beige skirt. A scarf wound around her neck gave her an ethereal look. When she looked up, the happy smile she gave him went straight to his heart. Then he caught Nana watching him, and he stifled his reaction.

He slipped back into the pew. Just as he put the Bible in the empty rack in front of him, the singing group came to the front and everyone got to their feet.

The first song was unfamiliar, as was the second one, but the music was light and uplifting. A couple of times he glanced over at Emma, who smiled as she sang, obviously caught up in the music.

The song finished and Emma glanced sidelong. As their gazes met, he felt it again. A connection. A sense that something could happen between them.

She seemed secure in her faith and as their eyes held, he endured a moment of envy. At one time he'd trusted God to watch over him and his family, but that trust was choked in the aftermath of Sylvia's and then Harry's death.

He yanked his gaze away from Emma. There was no future for them. She had a son. He'd had a son once, and he couldn't take care of him. Couldn't protect him.

Easier to stay alone.

The congregation sat down and the minister asked them to turn to the Bible. He pulled his out and opened it, holding it so Nana could read with him. She gave him a quick smile then put on her reading glasses.

"He who dwells in the shadow of the most high will dwell in the shelter of the Almighty. I will say of the Lord, 'He is my refuge and my fortress, my God, in whom I trust.'"

Those words caught Carter cold. He didn't trust God. Nor could he say he had found shelter in the Almighty.

He let the rest of the words of the psalm slip past him.

The Bible reading was over and the minister began his sermon. Carter leaned back in the pew, his eyes drifting over the familiar setting. Five hundred and eighty-five tiles in the ceiling. Twenty-five panes of green glass, thirty panes of yellow glass, forty panes of blue glass in the stained-glass windows. Everything the same as it was when he was a little kid, coming here every Sunday.

The minister's pulpit was in exactly the same place it had been since he was a kid. Cross behind him on the wall. Everything was the same as when Harry's coffin sat at the front of the church.

He yanked his gaze away, and his attention was snagged by Emma. She sat with her arm around Adam, whose head lay on her lap, his legs on the pew. He was sleeping. But her focus was on the minister. Her expression held an eager look, as if she took in everything he said and heard something Carter didn't.

He caught himself turning his own attention back to what the pastor was saying, wondering what caused that rapt look on Emma's face.

"God has never promised that we wouldn't have trouble, but He has promised to be alongside us in that trouble. So that we can, in the midsts of the storms of our life say with conviction, 'It is well with my soul,'" the pastor was saying. "We need to know more than anything that peace is not the absence of trouble in our lives—peace is the presence of God."

He spoke with such conviction that Carter caught himself clinging to his words, seeking some sliver of the elusive peace he had sought since Harry died. At one time he had trusted God. Did he dare trust Him again?

But what was the alternative? Chasing after work, after money—neither of which satisfied? Running away from the pain?

Carter looked down at his hands, now clasped tightly together. He wanted to believe God was at his side, that in His presence he could find peace. He wanted to trust God again.

He didn't know if he dared.

He chanced another look at Emma, wondering what she was thinking, and was surprised to see her looking at him. She gave him a careful smile, and his heart lifted in response.

She's pretty.

And she's not for you. You are on your own.

He tore his gaze away, thankful to hear the minister announce the closing song. He got up and sang along, but he couldn't shut his mind off to what the minister had said or to Emma's presence beside him.

Why did he have the feeling the two were intertwined?

She shouldn't have come to the family lunch.

Emma fussed with her scarf, all the while conscious of Carter sitting directly across from her. Once again she wished she had turned down Shannon's invitation to join the Beck family for lunch after church.

She tried to say no. However, Adam, lured on by Nana Beck with the promise of some new farm animals for the set he always played with, wouldn't let Emma refuse.

But now having Carter sitting right across from her was disconcerting and unsettling. The last time they'd shared a meal, it hadn't ended well.

And let's not forget your little lecture of last night.

Yet even as she acknowledged her cynical alter ego, another part of her felt something else was happening. Something a bit dangerous and, if she were completely honest with herself, a bit exciting.

He's a good-looking, hurting man. You're a lonely sympathetic person. Bad combination.

"Good message this morning, wasn't it?" Nana Beck was saying as Shannon spooned out the soup.

Silence followed that comment. Emma glanced from Carter to Shannon, feeling that it was their place to reply to the comment, not hers.

Carter's attention was on his bowl and Shannon tucked a strand of auburn hair behind her ear and sat down, fussing with her gold necklace.

"I especially appreciated how the minister said not the absence of trouble but that peace is the presence of God," Nana Beck continued, undaunted by the silence that greeted her.

Another pause followed, broken only by the clink of silverware on Nana Beck's china. Emma tried not to squirm in the uncomfortable quiet. She was sure Carter was thinking about his son and Shannon was thinking about the man who had left her just before their wedding.

"I know each of us sitting here at this table has had trials and doubts," Nana added, "but I like what the pastor was saying when he quoted C.S. Lewis. 'God whispers to us in our pleasures, speaks to us in our conscience, but shouts in our pains.' I know that I prefer to be whispered to."

More silence.

Emma couldn't take it anymore. "And yet at least for me, it has been in the hard places of my life, the moments I have struggled the hardest with God, that I have felt the closest to Him."

Nana Beck shot Emma a look of gratitude. "Isn't that true. I know that after both Sylvia's then Harry's deaths, I clung to God. Though I was angry with Him and hurt, I felt His nearness in a way I hadn't felt since my husband, Bill, died."

Emma sensed that Nana Beck's reference to Harry as well as Sylvia was deliberate, and while she buttered Adam's bun, she shot Carter a covert glance to see what his reaction was.

His features were unreadable.

"I know I question God at times," Shannon put in. "I wonder why things go the way they go…" Her voice faded away, and Nana Beck caught her arm and gave it a light shake.

"You are a beautiful woman, Shannon. And you deserve much better than what that snake Arthur did to you."

Shannon shook her head, as if dislodging her memories. "Gotta admit, it's a bit hard living in Hartley Creek knowing that I'm the cliché bride-almost-left-at-the-altar. But, my problems are small compared to some." Shannon gave Carter a meaningful glance, but his attention was still on the bowl in front of him.

"What new animals did you get for the farm?" Adam piped up, his completely unrelated question breaking the awkward silence after Shannon's comment.

"I got some goats and some chickens," Nana Beck said, relief entering her voice at the change in topic. "Some of them were missing, so I bought new ones."

"Did the boy lose them?" Adam asked, swirling his spoon through the soup, chasing down a meatball.

Emma handed him a bun and shot him a warning frown, but he wasn't looking at her. He was looking directly at Carter.

"You mean Harry?" Shannon asked.

Adam ducked his head, looking down at his bowl again. "Mom said I'm not 'sposed to talk about him," was his subdued response. "She said it hurts Mr. Carter, and I don't want him to be sad again."

The atmosphere around the table held a heavy expectancy, and Emma wished her son was less forthcoming.

"I'm sorry," Emma glanced around the table. "We had a talk about…and—"

"I'm not angry with you, Adam." Carter put his spoon down, folded his elbows on the table and leaned forward, his gray-blue eyes focused on Adam. "And I'm sorry if I made you feel that way."

Emma held her breath, her gaze flicking from Adam to Carter, wondering what her son would say next.

Adam pursed his lips, as if thinking. He chased down another meatball and fished it out of the soup. Then he shot Carter a shy glance. "It's okay. My mommy said sometimes it's better to talk about things. But if you don't want to talk about Harry, I'll keep my mouth shut."

Note to self: give Adam minimal information to save maximum embarrassment.

"No, you can keep talking, Adam." Carter's smile was cautious. "I like hearing what you have to say."

Adam perked up at that. "Do you like playing with the farm animals?"

Emma groaned inwardly. Every time they came to Nana Beck's for dinner or coffee, Adam tried to con someone into playing with the farm set.

Carter gave a light shrug. "I don't know. I guess I could find out."

"Do you know the rules?"

"Honey, Mr. Carter might not like playing by your rules," Emma said gently, throwing Carter a quick smile. Adam seemed willing to ignore any discomfort he felt with Carter to gain an unwitting player.

"I know the rules Harry used to use," Carter said.

Nana Beck pulled in a quick breath, and Emma saw her glance at Shannon as if to gain confirmation of what she had just heard. But Shannon's attention was riveted on Carter and Adam, her green eyes flicking from one to the other.

"What rules did your boy use?" Adam asked, oblivious to the heightened tension in the dining room.

"He always wanted the cows of all the same color to be together in a field," Carter said, crumbling his crackers into his soup. "And the sheep and goats had to be in their own pen."

"Because they are the same," Adam said, signaling his approval. "What did he do with the chickens?"

A melancholy smile drifted over his lips. "He kind of let the chickens go wherever they wanted."

Adam frowned and shook his head. "I never let the chickens do that."

Here come Adam's rules, Emma thought, opening her mouth to intervene. She felt a foot nudge her and glanced over to Nana Beck, who gave an imperceptible shake of her head.

As Adam listed out the reasons Harry had done it wrong, the corners of Carter's mouth quirked upward. Then he glanced at Emma. She couldn't look away, inwardly pleased at his reaction to Adam's prattling.

Then, to her confusion, she felt it again. The sense that

everything else slipped away in his presence. That she and he were the only people here.

She dragged her gaze away, feeling suddenly flustered. Unsure. This wasn't going the way she had pictured. This was dangerous. She shot a quick look at Adam, a visible reminder of her priority.

Carter is leaving. You are leaving. Focus on Adam.

"And the horses have to get water in the river because my mom says it's better for the horses," Adam was saying, swinging his legs back and forth as he warmed to his subject. "At my grandpa's ranch we had a big black tub to water the horses. When it was hot I would swim in it. You should get a big black tub for the horses. Then I can swim there because I can't swim in the river. Mom says it's too dangerous and I might drown."

Carter's lips had thinned at Adam's innocent prattle, and Emma knew her son had ventured too close to Carter's deepest pain.

"Are you finished with your soup?" She put her hand on Adam's shoulder and nudged his bowl toward him with her other hand, hoping he got the hint.

Adam ducked his head and picked up his spoon again. "Do I have to finish it all?"

"Yes. Otherwise you don't get dessert," Nana Beck said.

"How is the house hunting going?" Carter's voice held a strained note as he turned his attention back to his grandmother and cousin.

"We found a smallish house," Shannon said, breaking open her bun, shifting to a safer topic. "It's close to downtown and the doctor's office."

"It has an excellent view of the ski hill," Nana Beck put in. "Hailey will love it."

"Speaking of, is my cousin making the pilgrimage

home to see you, Nana?" Carter asked, his voice lightening and a smile lifting the corner of his mouth.

"She came to see me in the hospital," Nana said, her voice softening.

"Where is she now?" Carter asked.

"Working in Calgary," Shannon said.

"I wish she would come back to Hartley Creek," Nana Beck put in. "I know she loves it here." Nana shot Carter a frown. "She's going to be upset when she finds out that you're thinking of selling the ranch."

"I already talked to her, Nana. I even offered her a chance to buy the place herself."

Nana Beck snorted. "As if she could afford it on a teacher's salary." She sighed. "This place has been in our family for decades. I still can't believe—"

Shannon covered Nana Beck's hand with hers. "I know it's hard to understand, but Carter has to make up his own mind about the ranch."

Though she spoke quietly, Emma caught the glance Shannon sent Carter's way.

She felt bad for him. Though she agreed with Nana Beck, Shannon was right—it was still his decision to make and his ranch to sell or keep.

"I still think you're making a rash decision," Nana Beck said.

Carter eased out a sigh. "I'm sorry this isn't working out for you. But I can't stay here, and you want to move anyway."

Silence followed that comment.

"Before the ranch changes hands, we're going to have to organize a family get-together here," Shannon said. "Get everyone together one more time. Let us have a chance to remember old times."

It wasn't too hard to hear the melancholy tone in Shannon's voice, and Emma felt a twinge of sympathy for her and Nana Beck but also for Carter. He carried the weight of family history on his shoulders, and she sensed that the memories of each family member added to his burden.

"We've had lots of good memories here," Shannon added, cupping her hands around her mug. "Do you remember that time that Naomi and Hailey dressed up like ghosts?"

"Oh, my goodness, yes." Nana Beck shook her head, but she was smiling. "Garret screamed like a girl when he saw them rise up out of the pumpkin patch."

Laughter followed this memory.

"Then Garret got them back with that pail of water above their door, remember?" Carter said with a grin.

"Except I was the one that got drenched," Shannon said.

While the conversation skipped back and forth, recollections and old stories spilling out, Emma quickly finished up her lunch, encouraging Adam to do the same.

Though she knew all the names of Nana Beck's grandchildren and much of what they were doing, she sensed Carter, Shannon and Nana Beck would be more comfortable sharing family stories without her around.

"Thanks for lunch," she said, as soon as Adam finished the last of his soup and the bun she made him eat. She got up and brought their bowls to the counter. "Adam and I have to get going."

"But I want to play with the farm set," Adam said, wiping his mouth with his sleeve instead of the napkin.

"You can play with that another time." Emma shot him a warning glance.

"Nana Beck said she had some new animals and I didn't get dessert." His voice lifted toward the end of the sentence, coming dangerously close to whining territory.

"We can come back and play with the animals another time—"

"Nonsense. He can play with them now." Nana put her hand on Emma's arm when she came back to the table to get Adam. "I did tell him he could."

Emma was torn between keeping a promise to her son and wanting to let the Beck family spend time together without her, an interloper, around.

"I don't want to intrude," she said quietly.

"That's silly," Nana said with a frown.

Adam dragged at her hand. "Please, Mom? We can play in the living room. Real quiet."

Emma bit her lip, relenting. "Okay. Just for a little while, then we have to go."

Adam didn't wait for the rest of what she had to say. He was gone before she finished saying "Okay."

Emma followed him to the living room. Adam was pulling the box out of the bottom cupboard of the bookshelves.

As they laid out the farm set and Adam imposed his strict regimen, snatches of conversation slipped to the living room. Emma tried not to listen in, but part of her yearned for the connections and history Carter shared with his cousins. The banter and half-finished comments that didn't need to be completed because everyone knew the rest of the story.

Emma had grown up an only child who never got to know the grandparents who lived so far away. Her father had a sister who lived in Florida, also single. And that was it. The line of the family ended with her and Adam.

As she set out the pigs, according to Adam's Rules, she felt a twinge of regret. Growing up without siblings made her want a large family for her own children.

How things change, she thought, glancing at her dear

son. He was her entire focus. Her life. It was just the two of them.

In spite of that declaration, her thoughts slipped to Carter and the moments they spent together. That sense of heightened awareness that was often the precursor to something else. Something more.

The sound of Carter's laugh lifted her heart.

"What are you smiling at, Mom?" Adam poked her with a plastic cow, and she jerked herself back to her son and reality.

As she looked at his dear little face, a smear of butter still streaked across his cheek, she drew on a memory. The sight of his stricken expression when she told him that Karl wasn't going to be coming to the ranch anymore. The tears that welled up in his eyes when he discovered he wasn't going to get a father.

Emma hardened her heart, even as she heard Carter laughing again in the kitchen.

He was lonely. He was complicated.

And she had to stay away.

Chapter Eight

He was leaving again.

Emma rolled over in her bed, tucking the pillow under her cheek as the roar of Carter's motorbike faded away down the valley road into the night.

Even as she congratulated herself on her wisdom to keep her heart free from the complication that was Carter, part of her felt a surge of pity for his pain. Behind that pity came another, stronger emotion.

She flopped onto her back, pushing her feelings aside, forcing herself to focus on the job she had stayed to do. Tomorrow she would ride up to the upper pasture again.

Day after that, she and Adam had to go into town for a dentist's appointment, and she should get the mail which, inevitably, meant bills to pay and the tedium of filling out applications for another job.

After that they would have to think about cutting hay and baling it. Carter could probably run the hay bine to cut the hay. She could run the baler and rake.

But would the ranch be sold before all this happened?

She rolled back onto her side, struggling with her need to keep her mind busy and the concern that hung, ever present, on the edges of her mind.

And what would she do when the ranch sold? Where would she go? How would she take care of Adam? Would she have to sell Dusty and Diamond?

She dropped her hand over her eyes, sending up a prayer for…what? She wasn't sure.

Peace is not the absence of trouble, peace is the presence of God.

The quote from the pastor slipped into her mind, and behind that came another Bible passage she had read last night.

Peace I leave with you; my peace I give you. I do not give as the world gives. Do not let your hearts be troubled and do not be afraid.

Emma repeated the words, clinging to them. She had to trust that God would help her through this next phase of her life.

She repeated the Bible passage again, rolling over onto her side. Slowly, elusively, sleep found her. But just before she drifted off, her last thoughts were of slate-blue eyes and the sound of a motorbike's engine.

A light drizzle was falling when Carter strode across the yard toward his grandmother's house. The rain made it hard to tell exactly where the sun was, but Carter knew it was getting close to noon. He pulled the collar of his jacket up, wishing he had his oilskin.

He'd slept in this morning and woke up only when he heard rain on the roof of his cabin. A quick glance at his watch had shown him it was already close to noon.

He knocked on the door of his grandmother's house, then toed his boots off. He pulled off his hat, shook off the excess water then stepped inside.

Nana Beck sat on her couch, her Bible in her lap. The

sight created a flicker of guilt as he thought of the still-unopened Bible sitting beside his bed.

"How nice to see you, my dear," Nana said, motioning for him to come closer. He brushed his damp hair back, bent over and gave her a quick kiss, then gave her hands an extra squeeze.

"Goodness, your hands are cold," she said. "Do you want a cup of tea?"

"No. I had breakfast." He didn't respond to the questioning lift of her eyebrow or her quick glance at the clock. "Just wondering if you've seen Emma this morning."

Guilt stalked his every step. Last night he gave up on sleeping and had gone for a ride on his bike. He came home late and as a result had slept in. Emma's cabin was empty when he knocked on her door. She wasn't in the barn, the tack shed or the main farmhouse. Her truck was still parked in front of the machine shed by her horse trailer.

Nana frowned and shook her head. "She did say something about picking beans when she came back, though I doubt she will in this rain."

"Back? From where?"

"I'm not sure. I was taking in my clothes from the line when she and Adam came by on the horses."

"Horses?"

Nana frowned at him. "No need to sound snappy, my boy. I'm just telling you what happened."

Carter gave his grandmother an apologetic smile. "Sorry, Nana. I'm concerned. It's raining out and I can't figure where she would go on horses in this wet weather."

A smile eased away Nana's frown. "I don't think you need to worry about Emma. She's capable and independent. She's been a big help to Wade on the ranch. I think she really loves it here."

Carter saw his grandmother fold her hands on her Bible. Usually a sign that some type of lecture or scolding was coming his way.

"Shannon told me that you listed the ranch already?"

Carter thought they had covered all this yesterday over lunch. "Yes. I did. And Pete already found a buyer."

"Why so soon? Why so quick? You've only been back a few days, and you're making this huge decision?" Nana Beck's fingers tightened around each other.

Carter steeled himself to the pain in her voice. "I wanted to do this after…two years ago, Nana. As long as you still lived here, I wasn't making you move out of your home."

"But this is your home too."

The catch in her voice hooked into his heart.

Last night, as he shifted and sighed in his bed, seeking elusive sleep, he struggled with his decision. Coming back to the ranch had been harder than he thought.

Talking about Harry yesterday, first with Matt at church, then Adam, then with Shannon and Nana, had brought out painful memories. Yet, in spite of the pain, he was surprised it hadn't hurt more.

The biggest surprise was finding out how much he missed having someone to share memories with. Reliving old stories and escapades eased out good memories of the ranch. Memories he had also suppressed.

He didn't blame Emma for slipping out with Adam while the Becks made a trek down memory lane, but he wished Emma had stayed longer. He enjoyed her company and, in spite of his own sorrow, talking about Harry, even for a moment, had helped as she had said it would.

Last night, while he lay awake, twisting and turning

in his bed, an errant thought slinked around the edges of his mind. Was selling the ranch a selfish move?

He looked out the rain-streaked window of Nana's house to the corral. The horse trough was gone, but the memory wasn't. And on the heels of that memory, the guilt swept in.

He couldn't live with these reminders every day.

He shoved his hand through his hair as he exhaled heavily. "I'm sorry, Nana. I feel like I should put this part of my life behind me. It hurts too much."

Nana's eyes brimmed with tears as she got up. "I'm so sorry for you, my boy. I've been praying every day that you would be able to live with the memories. That you would forgive yourself. When you said you were coming back, I was so hoping you would stay."

Carter picked up his hat and turned it around in his hands, his second thoughts of last night niggling at him. "I really feel I need to move on." He bent over and gave her another kiss. "I'd better see if I can find Emma and Adam. Find out why she didn't let me know what she was doing." He didn't want to admit this to his grandmother, but he was a bit worried

"Give her a little slack," Nana said quietly. "She's used to doing a lot on her own."

"Maybe she has, but she should still let me know when she's going to be gone."

"Of course she should."

Did he imagine that little smirk on his grandmother's face?

"By the way, have you heard anything from Wade?" she asked, thankfully moving on to another topic.

"Yeah, he called me on my cell phone. His father is in stable condition, but his mother will need some surgery. Wade is doing okay, but he's a little frazzled."

His grandmother clucked in sympathy. "Then we'll need to remember them in our prayers."

Carter felt a twinge of envy. Prayers. It had been some time since he had talked to God other than in anger. He wished he could be as trusting as his grandmother seemed to be about God's listening ear.

"You do that, Nana. Meantime, I better go see what Emma has been up to."

"Don't you be getting angry with her," Nana admonished.

Carter couldn't help a faint smile at his grandmother's defense of Emma.

"I won't." He dropped his hat on his head and strode across the yard to the tack shed.

He snagged a halter off a peg, then headed to the horse pasture. He whistled for the horses, but they didn't come.

Frowning, he climbed over the fence and walked toward them.

Banjo lifted his head at Carter's approach. Then, with a whinny, he turned and trotted in the opposite direction.

The other horses whinnied, then followed their leader.

He whistled again, but Banjo wasn't listening.

"Ungrateful critter," he muttered, threading the halter rope through his hands. He watched the horses, figuring his next move. He wasn't going to chase them around the pasture. The trick was to get the horses to come to him.

Just as he was planning his strategy, the horses stopped, whinnied and trotted toward the fence.

Carter looked in the same direction and saw Emma and Adam on their horses, coming down the trail from the upper pasture.

"Hey, Mr. Carter," Adam called out, the leather of his saddle squeaking, standing in his stirrups as they approached. His bright yellow jacket and black pants made him look like a bumblebee. "Did you finally wake up?"

The "finally" cut. A bit. But Carter just nodded.

The horses came alongside and Emma reined them in. She wore a brown cowboy hat today and an oilskin jacket and worn leather chaps. Water dripped off her hat, but she was smiling.

Carter's mind flashed back to a trip he had made with Sylvia when they first were married. They had ridden up and around the hills behind the ranch, and it began to rain. Sylvia, normally easygoing, had complained all the way down. When they got back she said she wasn't going out riding again unless Carter could guarantee sunny weather.

Emma, however, didn't seem daunted by the moisture or the fact that she had mud spatters on her chaps, coat and face.

"Where did you go?" he asked, forcing his attention back to the subject he wanted to talk to her about.

"Up to the higher pasture. Didn't you read the note I put on your door?"

Carter frowned. He hadn't bothered to check his door. Didn't even think she might have left him a note.

"No. I didn't."

"I think we'll have to move the cows in a few days. I wanted to make sure they were okay until then."

"Why didn't you wake me up?" He set his hands on his hips, trying to look as if he was in charge.

"I heard you leave late last night. I thought you would still be tired." She gave him a careful smile as she dismounted.

Carter sighed as a trickle of rain worked its way down his back. "You're my ranch hand, not my mother."

The edge in his voice came from a mixture of frustration with a horse he couldn't catch and guilt that this woman and her son were able to take care of his ranch without him.

At any rate, his curt tone made her smile disappear and her lips thin. He felt like a heel. His grandmother had just warned him about getting angry with her.

"Okay. Next time I'll ask before I make the same decisions I've been making since I was hired." Her voice took on a prim tone. She swiped a gloved hand across the moisture trickling down her face, smearing the bits of mud across her cheek. Which ruined the confident and in-charge effect he guessed she was going for.

Which in turn made him smile.

She glared at him, her brown eyes snapping. "What's so funny, Carter? Is it so hard to imagine me in charge?"

"No. Not at all. It's just—" How was he to regroup from this?

"I've been taking care of the cows since I got here," she said, gripping Diamond's reins, not giving him a chance. "The whole pasture-management scheme was mine. Wade, thankfully, was able to trust me to do what I'd been doing for four years on my father's ranch. I know what I'm doing."

He held up his hand in a placating gesture. Where did this prickly attitude come from? "I'm not a chauvinist, Emma. I appreciate what you've done here. It just felt weird to get up and find out you were off doing what I should have been doing."

She blinked, glancing back at Adam, who was still on his horse, a puzzled frown pulling his eyebrows together.

"Again. I'm sorry," she mumbled. "I thought since you're selling the place, it wouldn't matter what I did..." She let the sentence trail off.

"I'm selling this place as a turnkey operation, and I

want to make sure that I know what's happening on the ranch when I talk to the potential buyer."

Even as he mouthed those words, a part of his mind accused him of lying. No, the reason he cared went deeper. Went back to his youth. To growing up on this place. To all the memories that were such a part of him and had only recently come out again. The memories he had from before Harry died.

"Speaking of the buyer," Emma said, her voice lowering. "Did you find anything out about subdividing the acreage from the new owner?"

Carter rubbed his chin, feeling a flicker of regret as he recalled his last conversation with Pete. "Apparently the new owner wants to keep the land untouched. He likes the isolation and isn't interested in breaking off parcels of the ranch." He caught the sorrow in her eyes. "I'm sorry, Emma. I wish I could tell you something different."

"That's okay." Emma's quiet words showed Carter how much of a disappointment this was to her. But he could do nothing. It was out of his hands.

She turned away and walked over to her son to help him out of the saddle. As soon as Adam's feet hit the ground, he scooted over to Carter, eyes bright. "My mom said that if the weather is nice, when we go to move the cows, we're going to have a picnic."

Carter knelt down so that he was face-to-face with him. "A picnic sounds like a great idea," he said, giving the boy a quick smile.

Adam put his hand on Carter's shoulder. "Can you come with us?"

The touch of Adam's hand created a mixture of emotions. Sorrow for his lost son, but also a connection with this little boy who looked at him with such trust.

"That would be nice," he said quietly, holding Adam's

gaze. Then, as if of its own will, Carter's hand reached up and covered Adam's. To his surprise the sorrow eased away, replaced by a surprising tenderness toward Adam.

Adam's grin lit up his mud-streaked face. "Maybe my mom will let me take pop."

"That would be nice too," Carter said. He pointed at Adam's face. "But you're going to have to wash your face before we go."

Adam frowned then lifted his shoulder and wiped a trickle of water off his cheek, making the smear bigger. "Is it gone?"

Carter laughed then pulled out his hanky and wiped Adam's cheek. Then as he straightened, he caught Emma smiling at him, her eyes soft.

As their gazes held, his emotions shifted into a new place. A question arose in his mind. Could they...

His first reaction was to withdraw. But the question wouldn't go away.

Then he gave in to an impulse and reached over and gently wiped the mud off her face, as well. "There. Now you're all clean too." As he gave her a wink, he took advantage of her momentary bewilderment to gather up the reins of the horses and lead them away.

"So you pay the bills online now?" Carter asked, frowning at the computer.

Emma moved the mouse, gave it a click and tried not to notice how close Carter sat. He had to, she reasoned, to see the monitor better, but it still was too close for her comfort.

She smelled the rain on his clothes, the faint scent of horses on his blue jeans.

The hint of spicy aftershave lotion from his cheeks.

The same smell that was on the hanky he used to wipe her face. Why had he done that?

She swallowed and forced her attention back to the computer. Focus. Focus.

"Our banker told us it was perfectly safe," Emma said opening the banking site and plugging in the password. She had to try three times before she got it right.

"All the account information is here." Emma hit the Okay button again. Thankfully this time it was right and a new screen flashed up on the monitor.

In the background she heard the soundtrack of the movie Adam was watching. A bribe so she could pay the bills she had picked up in town this morning.

One of the reasons she had gone to town was to get the mail she knew would be piling up. The other was to look for a place to live, a job and a place to board her horses.

The easiest part of the excursion was getting the mail. Three of the jobs she had circled in the newspaper from the week before were filled. The fourth place was looking for someone with more education than she had. Not one of the jobs was in her field of expertise—horses and ranching.

She had tried to let go of her concern and hope that something, somewhere would come up.

"And working on this site is safe?" Carter asked as she clicked into the checking account.

He reached across her and pulled a pen out of the holder in front of her.

Droplets of moisture were captured in the waves of his thick hair. She had to clench her fists to keep herself from brushing them away.

What was wrong with her? Why was she so jumpy around him lately?

So aware of him?

"Emma? Did you hear me?"

She jerked her attention back to the computer screen and away from him. "Yeah. I did. Sorry. It's perfectly safe." She drew in a quick breath. "Plus it's convenient. Much easier to do this way. We don't have to get to town on time to meet the deadlines. It also saves a bunch of postage, which all helps. But, yeah, the bank account is well, healthy."

And you are babbling like an idiot.

Carter shot her a puzzled look. "Why are you so nervous?"

"I'm not nervous," she said with a shaky laugh.

"You talk more when you are."

Emma took refuge in sarcasm. "So now you're the Emma expert?"

Carter said nothing, and the only sounds in the ensuing silence were strains of music coming from the living room. Sounded as if the movie was ending.

He held her gaze, and a faint smile curved up one corner of his mouth. "What's wrong, Emma?"

You're what's wrong, she wanted to say. *You're a distraction and a problem.* Her son in the next room was a potent reminder of what was at stake for her if she made bad choices. He depended on her to take care of him.

Getting distracted by an attractive, wounded man was not in Adam's best interests. Especially not a man who had no intention of sticking around.

Been there. Done that.

"I've just got...things on my mind." She caught herself. No whining, either.

Carter leaned an elbow on the table but didn't look away. "Like what?"

She kept her eyes on the computer screen. "It's not your worry." She clicked on the Pay Bill button and flipped through the bills in front of her, looking for the next one to pay.

"Is it a job you're worried about? Your future?"

Her hand paused. The concern in his voice was almost her undoing. How long had it been since anyone, including her father and even Karl, her once-fiancé, had even been concerned about her? Had cared enough to ask?

"It's a factor," she said, pulling out the envelope she was looking for and ripping it open. "I'll be fine. I can manage."

"You do that well," Carter said quietly.

"Open envelopes?" she asked, deliberately misunderstanding him.

"Act like everything is fine. Like you're in control."

Emma clutched the paper then lowered it to the desk trying to mask her awareness of him. "I've never believed I'm in control. I don't think any of us are."

Just look at him. Act as if you're not aware of his height. The breadth of his shoulders.

The largeness of him that made a girl feel safe. Protected.

That's a pipe dream, and you know it. You can't trust men.

"No, I don't suppose we are," Carter said quietly, looking directly at her. Then he tilted his mouth up in a smile and, to her surprise and dismay, reached over and brushed his fingers over her cheek.

She tried to stop the rush of warmth washing up her neck, heating her cheeks. He had done that before. When he wiped the mud off her face. What was he trying to do to her?

"You had a piece of lint stuck to your face," he said, holding up his fingers to show her.

"Oh. I see." She turned back to the computer, hoping

he didn't notice her shaking fingers. She typed in a number in the box to pay the bill, corrected it and tried again.

"So then, once the bill is paid, I enter the amount in the checkbook," she said quietly, hoping she sounded in control. In charge. "That way, if Wade takes the checkbook to town, he knows exactly how much is still in the account."

"That's easier than the way I did it," he said with a rueful grin. "Sylvia always said I did things backward."

Emma was surprised. This was the first time she'd heard him mention his wife's name. "Did she ever do the books?"

Carter laughed and shook his head. "She was a good woman, but she always said she could add up four numbers five times and come up with six different answers."

"I saw a picture of her at Nana Beck's," she said, capitalizing on his memory. "She was a beautiful woman."

Carter's sigh held more melancholy than sadness. "She was. Inside and out. She was a real example to me of Christian love. I sometimes wonder what Harry would have been like if she'd been around." A tiny break entered his voice as he spoke of his son.

His sorrow touched Emma's nurturing soul. She reached over and covered his hand with hers.

"I'm so sorry, Carter," she said quietly. "Sorry for all you've lost."

He held her gaze and gave her a wistful smile as his hand squeezed hers in return. "I'm sorry too."

Their gazes held again. But she felt a shift in the atmosphere. A change from sadness to something deeper.

Attraction. Understanding. A sense of coming home.

Look away. Look away. This is trouble.

But Emma couldn't.

"Mom, the movie is done," Adam announced, hopping

into the kitchen and bringing energy, enthusiasm and reality with him.

Emma yanked her hands away from Carter's and swallowed down the anticipation brewing in her chest.

"Can I have a cookie?" Adam asked.

Emma nodded absently, furiously clicking on another button, suddenly wishing Carter would let her finish up alone.

Adam wandered to her side and wiggled his way between Emma and Carter, his hands full of cookies. "Can I sit on your lap, Mom?" he asked.

"In a minute, buddy." She frowned at the cookies in his hand. "Why did you take four?"

He laid two on the desk. "One for you and one for Mr. Carter."

"Two for you, I noticed," Carter said with a surprising grin.

"Yup. 'Cause I'm the cookie getter." Adam took a bite of his cookie and released a dramatic sigh. "How come I can't sit on your lap?"

"Because I can't work on the computer and hold you at the same time."

"I can't see." Adam turned to Carter. "Can I sit on your lap? Sometimes, when Mommy is done on the computer she lets me play a game. Or look at the horse pictures."

Emma's gaze flew to Carter, even as she nudged her son, hoping to catch his attention. She wished she had let Adam sit on her knees, because she knew Carter would turn him down.

But Carter was looking at Adam, his mouth curved in a rueful smile.

Then, to her surprise and amazement, he lifted Adam up on his lap.

As Adam settled against Carter, Emma felt a whirlwind of emotions. Astonishment that Carter would willingly take Adam and hold him.

And, threaded through that, a sense of confusion she couldn't pin down. She didn't want Adam to connect with Carter this way. She didn't want her son to be tied in with the man who was, even now, making Emma's hands clumsy and making her heart lift. The scene was too much like a family setting. Mother, father, son. All cozy and comfortable.

Guarding her heart was how she had to take care of Adam. Carter was outrunning his past by leaving when the ranch sold. This would never work. Adam could not experience another disruption in his young life.

"When you're finished can we look at the pictures?" Adam was saying.

"Yes. And then you can sit on my lap," she said with a false brightness as she slit open another envelope. She flew through the rest of the bills, flipping and clicking and hoping she input the correct amounts. She wanted to be done so she could split up this too-cozy tableau.

She closed the bank site then opened up the photo program. Wade had made a file of horse pictures, and Adam loved looking at them.

But her hands were clumsy and she hit the wrong file. As she reached for Adam, a movie opened up. A little boy waved at the camera from on top of a horse.

Harry.

Wade led the horse and in the background Emma heard Carter's voice, probably from behind the camera. "Make sure you hold on, Harry. Don't show off too much."

The movie showed Wade bringing Harry closer to the camera, and Emma couldn't look away even as she clicked and clicked, trying to shut the program down.

Harry was a younger version of Carter. Same thick, wavy hair. Same blue eyes. Same crooked smile.

She heard a sharp intake of breath from Carter and then…finally…thankfully, the movie disappeared. An intense silence followed. Emma was sure everyone heard the heavy pounding of her heart.

Then Adam turned to Carter. "I'm sad that your little boy can't be here." The simple words slashed the quiet.

Emma was afraid to look at Carter, to see his reaction. But her gaze slipped to his face anyway, and to her surprise, moisture glimmered in his eyes.

"I'm sad too," was all Carter said, his voice quiet.

"Maybe if you pray, God will help you feel better," Adam replied with the simple confidence of his innocent faith.

Carter's smile was warm and Emma's heart tumbled in her chest as Carter brushed his hand over Adam's hair. "Maybe," he said. Then he gently set Adam aside, mumbled a hurried "Excuse me," and left.

When the door clicked behind him, Emma felt tears prick her eyelids. Seeing Carter's son, alive and smiling, made his loss tangible. Painful.

What must Carter be going through right now?

Ten minutes later she got the answer as she heard the rumble of Carter's motorbike starting up then, in spite of the rain, leaving.

His life is too messy, she reminded herself, stifling the momentary attraction she had just experienced. *Adam doesn't need more complications and disappointments. You're the only one who can take care of him.*

Yet, even as she talked herself through her usual litany, a yearning for the momentary connection she and Carter shared thrummed through her.

What was she supposed to do about that?

Chapter Nine

"Can we take some cookies along?" Adam leaned on the counter watching Emma making sandwiches.

It was early morning, and she and Adam were putting together the picnic in Miranda and Wade's house—Carter's old house, she thought.

"Sorry, buddy, they're all gone," she said absently, half her attention on her son, the other on how many sandwiches she should make. "But you can take some chips."

Yesterday, after Carter left, the rain quit and the sun came out, promising a better day. Today they had to go up to move the cows. She could only assume Carter was coming along. Especially after his speech about him still being the owner of the ranch.

Would the situation be awkward?

"But I really like cookies," Adam grumped. "So can I take pop instead?"

"Why don't we take our water bottles?" she suggested. "That way if you empty it, you can fill the bottle up in the stream." Thankfully Adam didn't counter that offer.

To make up for the lack of cookies, Emma put in an extra bag of chips and added two more chocolate bars.

A quick glance at the clock showed her she had time to spare.

"Let's go and see Nana Beck," she said, lifting Adam off the chair. "Make sure she's doing okay."

"Why is Nana moving off the ranch?" Adam asked as Emma pushed the chair back under the table.

"She's not been feeling well and she wants to live closer to the hospital, which means moving to town."

"I don't think she should move." Adam shoved his hands in his pockets and shot Emma a petulant look. "I don't think we should move."

Emma's heart faltered at the sadness in her son's voice. She knelt down and brushed his hair back from his face, then wiped a remnant of breakfast from the corner of his mouth. "Things change, son. And Mr. Carter is selling the ranch."

"Can't we work for the other man? The man buying the ranch?"

Emma thought of what Carter had told her about the acreage then, with a light sigh, shook her head. "Sorry, Adam. I want to find a place where we can live for good. A place we can own."

Adam frowned. "We have a place to live. The cabin."

"It's not the same." He was only five. He didn't understand the need to put down roots. The need to have a place no one could take away. He trusted her to take care of that for him.

She gave him a quick kiss to forestall more questions then pushed herself to her feet. "Let's go see Nana Beck." Then find Carter.

They stepped out into warm, inviting sunshine, so welcome after two days of drizzle and rain. Adam ran ahead of her, singing at the top of his lungs some song he had learned at Sunday school.

He flapped his arms, turning in circles, laughing at his own antics. The sight of him running so free gave her heart a tug. Come September he'd be going to kindergarten. After that, full-time school.

She wanted to stop time and bottle it. To hold these moments close. He was her precious little boy, and she wanted to keep him to herself as long as she could.

"Someone is in a good mood."

Emma jumped at the sound of Carter's voice behind her. He had caught up to her, his hands in the pockets of an old oilskin jacket, chaps covering his legs.

"We still on for moving the cows?" he asked, shooting her a sidelong glance.

Emma tried to gauge his mood. She hadn't seen him since he left yesterday. When he had finally returned, it was 7:00 p.m. and he had gone directly to Nana Beck's house.

Now, he acted as if yesterday hadn't happened.

"I was taking Adam to see if Nana Beck needed anything," she said, trying to keep her voice casual. "Then I was going to get you."

He held up a hand, as if to stop her. "Don't worry. I won't run the old 'I'm the owner of this ranch' schtick like I did the last time."

She nodded, slipping her hands in her pockets, unsure of what she should say. Then she figured, go with ordinary. Act as if nothing happened.

"So where were you just now?" she asked, glancing at the water beaded up on his leather chaps.

"I took Elijah out for a ride. Figured he needed a bit of extra work. We went down the trail leading to the river."

"You thinking of taking him along this morning?"

"When we go move the cows?" Carter shook his head,

his eyes still on Adam. "For that I'll need a more seasoned horse. Which one works better with your horses?"

She angled him a questioning look, wondering if he was just trying to make her feel important after her little spiel of the other day.

"Banjo. Definitely," she said, playing along for now. "Plus, he's more docile, which is better with the cows."

"In other words, a plug."

Emma laughed as she walked up the steps to Nana Beck's house. "I wasn't going to say that, but—"

"He won't win the Triple Crown." Carter finished her sentence.

Their eyes met and humor flashed between them. "He's a good horse. Solid and dependable. Which is more important in my books than flash and dash."

Carter's mouth curved into a crooked smile. "That's good to know."

Then as she reached for the door, he caught her by the shoulder and turned her back to face him. Emma fought the urge to pull back, sensing he wanted to tell her something.

"I want to apologize for taking off yesterday and leaving you with the books. It was just…" His slate-blue eyes held hers, and in their depths she saw his pain. At the same time, she caught something else. Something she couldn't define.

"I understand," she said quietly, carefully stepping back from him. "I'm so sorry about the movie. I can't imagine how hard it was to see Harry that way."

He slowly drew in a breath, looking away from her. "I didn't expect…didn't think I'd see him, hear him…" His voice broke and Emma's heart broke too.

"He looked like you," she said quietly.

Carter nodded then released a short laugh, but it didn't

have the same bitter tone it would have the first time she met him. "My cousin Shannon always said Harry looked more like me than Garret did. Though Sylvia's mom and dad said he looked like Sylvia's father."

"I guess a person sees who they want to see."

"So who do people say Adam looks like?"

His question created a twinge of envy. "He doesn't look much like me or my father, but neither does he look like his father. Of course, I have no clue if he looks anything like Adam's grandfather. I never met him."

Carter frowned, and in that moment she felt a deep sense of shame at her messy past.

She lifted her shoulder in what she hoped was a casual shrug. "When Adam's father found out I was pregnant, he took off. I haven't gotten so much as a phone call or text message from him or his family since then."

"I'm sorry," he said, lightly touching her shoulder. She wanted to feel comforted, but instead it brought out the stark contrast between her and Sylvia. Sylvia who had family and community.

Emma, who had a sordid and shameful past as compared with Carter's history and roots.

She pushed the memory and comparisons aside. "So who do you think Harry looked like?" she asked, moving back to their previous topic.

"I always thought he looked more like Naomi, my other cousin," Carter said, a pensive smile curving his lips.

"Naomi of the middle cabin?"

"That Naomi." Carter pulled his hat off his head then gave her a quick smile.

Emma shook her head, deliberately keeping her tone light. "I haven't met Naomi, but if Harry looked liked her, then she is more your twin than Garret is."

Carter's laugh was genuine. "Garret and I don't look that much alike for twins."

"I noticed that."

"Where?"

"In the pictures Nana has up on the wall." Nana Beck had an entire gallery devoted to her family, though pictures of the grandchildren far outnumbered the pictures of her daughters, Denise and Noelle.

"You've seen the photos?"

"And the albums," Emma said, adding a wink. "I know all your secrets."

Carter laughed again. Then, as their gazes met, a mellow smile still tugged up one corner of his mouth. "Thanks. For listening. For letting me talk. It's been hard, coming back. But the past few days have been… interesting. Don't know how else to say it. Seeing Harry yesterday was tough, but somehow, not as tough as I'd imagined."

"I'm thinking you've never had a chance to talk about him. Any of the people you've been around didn't know him and even if they did know you lost a son, they couldn't empathize."

"But you can."

"I know loss," she said softly. "But I haven't had to deal with what you've had to. I'm sure it's been a long, hard road for you the past few years."

Carter shook his head slowly. "When Sylvia died I thought that God gave me my quota of pain. Guess not."

"I don't think a God who promises us that He will always be with us is a God who doles out pain and sorrow."

Carter shrugged at that. Then he touched her shoulder again. It was a simple graze of his hand, but it sent a tingle down her spine. "Thanks for listening and for talking. You seem to know what to say, when."

His quiet words settled into her soul.

She waited, then unsure of what to say next, she opened the door of Nana Beck's house. After toeing off her boots, she followed Adam's happy chatter and the homey smell of cookies baking to the kitchen.

Adam had already pushed a chair against the counter, supervising Nana Beck removing cookies from the cookie sheet.

"Are some of them for us?" he asked, his chubby elbows planted on the counter as he watched. "Because we don't have any cookies for our picnic, and I really like cookies."

"Of course some of them are for you. You can't have a picnic without cookies." Nana turned, and her blue eyes lit up behind her glasses when she saw Carter and Emma. "So you two finally came in."

You two. As if they were a couple.

Emma dismissed the little tingle her words gave her and beckoned to Adam. "We have to get the horses ready, mister."

Adam glanced from Emma to Carter. "Is Mr. Carter coming with us?"

"We can't move those cows by ourselves," Emma said.

Adam pumped a fist in celebration. "We get to have cookies," he announced as he scooted off the chair. Then he turned to Nana, a worried look on his face. "Do the cookies have to cool or can we take them now?"

Nana Beck held up a paper bag. "I packed some already for you guys." She handed them to Adam. "Now you make sure they don't get broken, or they won't taste as good."

"That's silly," Adam said. "My mommy says that if a cookie is broken, you get more to eat."

"Are you going to be okay?" Emma asked Nana Beck as Adam opened the bag and counted the number of cookies inside.

"I'm feeling great. I had an urge to do some baking. I'll sit down after this." She wiped her hands on a rag, looking from Emma to Carter then to Adam. "Shannon is bringing me lunch this afternoon, so I won't be by myself for very long."

"Okay, then," Emma said. "You have a good day." She turned to Carter. "I'll get our lunch and meet you at the corrals."

His smile was simply to acknowledge what she said, but it still gave her spirits a peculiar quiver.

She put her hand on Adam's head, still bent over the bag, and steered him toward the porch. As they walked to the house, her footsteps quickened and her smile grew, though she didn't want to analyze why.

"Is there power on the line?" Emma's voice drifted across the open field.

Carter looked down at the tester that he had just put against the electric wire he and Emma had spent an hour stringing up as a fence for the cows. "Full power," he called back.

He gathered up the tester and put it back in his saddlebag, waiting for Emma. She got on her horse and rode toward him, glancing back now and again at the cows they had just moved.

Her hat hung from her neck by a leather strap. The wind picked up her hair, tossing it around her face. Carter smiled at how natural she looked sitting on that horse.

When they herded the cows to the other field, it was

sheer pleasure to see her horse responding to her slight shifts in the saddle, her gentle touch on the reins and the nudges of her feet on her horse's side. All smoothly done without flash or dash, as she had said earlier.

While she rode she lowered the reins, gathered her hair up and tied it back in a ponytail with a few quick twists.

Too bad. Carter liked it better when she let her hair down, when it framed her face in loose, brown waves.

He buckled up the saddlebag, trying to stifle his response to her. For the past few days he'd catch himself thinking about her. Worrying about her and her son, and what they would do once he sold the ranch. Adam so clearly loved being on the ranch. It bothered him to think of the little guy living in town.

Yesterday, after getting over seeing Harry in the video, he'd gone into town, to see Pete at the real estate office.

Things were coming together, Pete had told him. The buyer's financing had come through, but Carter still had a few days to stop the deal. If he didn't come into the office to sign the paper revoking the sale by the date and time set out in the agreement, then it was a done deal, Pete reminded him.

Now, standing up on the mountain, watching Emma come toward him on the horse, looking as if she belonged here, the second thoughts shadowing him were gaining substance.

She fit here. He realized that what he felt for her was deeper than mere looks. She was a devoted mother, a hard worker. A caring person. And his attraction to her increased each moment they spent together.

A tempting thought drifted on the edge of his consciousness.

What if he stayed? What if he changed his mind about selling the ranch?

He caught himself as Emma pulled up beside him.

"I think we have some very happy cows," Emma said as she swung down from the saddle. "They should be good for a couple of weeks yet. All that rain certainly helped."

"I can't believe how much grass we still have up here," Carter said, resting an arm on the pommel of his saddle. He dragged his gaze away from her, back to the cows.

Their red-brown bodies gleamed in the sun, sleek and fat, as they munched on the new grass. The calves raced around, checking out the perimeter of this new pasture. One touched the fence, let out a throaty bawl and then raced back toward its mother, the rest of the calves right behind. Carter laughed at the sight.

"That's what the rotational grazing has done," Emma said, threading the reins of her horse through her hand. "Next year I'd hoped to find a different way to feed the cows the hay over the winter. I've done some research on it—" She caught herself and looked away. "Anyhow, it was a good theory."

"We can have our picnic here," Adam called out from the copse of trees he'd been scouting out for the past few minutes.

"Shall we go?" Emma asked, picking up Dusty's reins from where Adam had dropped them. Without a backward look, she led both horses away.

In a matter of minutes Emma had a blanket spread out and was handing Adam various containers.

"Is there anything I can do?" Carter asked.

"We've got it under control." Emma glanced up at him then away, as if she was suddenly awkward around him. All the way up here she'd been quiet, and he wondered if he'd said too much on the porch.

He tied up the horses, and when he came back it looked as if everything was ready.

Carter sat down on the edge of the blanket, glancing from Emma to Adam. What were they waiting for?

"So. We're here. Let's pray," Emma said, nudging Adam. He pulled his cowboy hat off and Carter, surprised at this little moment, followed suit.

"Thank You, Lord, for the beautiful sunshine and the rain," Emma prayed. "Thank You for smoothing our path as we moved the cows. Thank You for this food and for a chance to be outside in Your amazing creation. Help us in our times of sadness and sorrow to know that You take care of us. Amen."

Carter kept his head lowered a moment, moved by her prayer. Simple yet sincere. Comfortable even. He felt close to God as she had prayed.

"So, here are the sandwiches. I didn't know what kind you liked, so I made a variety," Emma was saying as she snapped the lids off containers. "There's water in a bottle for you."

"If you need more to drink, you can take it out of the creek," Adam said. "But you don't want to go where the cows go. Because that's gross."

"Of course it is," Carter said with a grin, taking a sandwich out of the container. He took a bite and smiled at Emma. "Miranda had some homemade bread left?"

"Actually, I made it."

"Really?"

"Why do you sound surprised?" An injured tone crept into her voice.

"Sorry. I assumed that you were more of an animal person than a domestic one," Carter said, trying to backpedal and failing miserably. Animal person? Really?

"I kept house for me and my father," Emma replied, taking a bite out of her sandwich. "I can do domestic too."

"It's just you're so good with horses and animals, I can't see you with an apron on working in the kitchen." He stopped there and finished off his sandwich in the awkward silence. Then he dusted off the crumbs from his shirt and heaved a sigh. "Okay, I think no matter what I do I'm going to say the wrong thing here. So why don't I just apologize in advance and hope it covers any other dumb thing I might say for the rest of the afternoon."

Her burst of laughter was a welcome surprise.

"It's okay. I shouldn't be so touchy. So I apologize too."

"Is there a best-before date on your apology? I'm wondering if it will cover the next few weeks of dumb things Carter might say.'"

This netted him some more laughter. Which brought out a sparkle in her eyes and a flush in her cheeks.

Which made her even more attractive than before.

He turned his attention back to the lunch spread out before him.

"So Adam, what should I have next?"

Adam tapped his fingers on his chin, considering. Then he picked up another container. "My mom's potato salad is really good."

"Potato salad it is, cowboy."

As they ate, any previous discomfort faded and the conversation drifted along. Adam told Carter about the tree house. Emma and Carter talked about the calf crop. The hay crop. Nana Beck's health. Carter's family.

Halfway through the conversation Adam moved onto his side, closed his eyes and promptly fell asleep. Emma shifted off the blanket and covered him up with the rest of it.

"He didn't sleep well last night," Emma said quietly,

getting up. "I'd like to move away so we don't wake him." She walked over to a large spruce tree and sat down.

Adam snorted and Emma looked back, checking on him, but he settled down again and soon they could hear his heavy, steady breathing.

"Sorry about this," Emma said quietly. "I knew he was tired, but he insisted on coming along. I'd kinda like to let him sleep for a bit, if that's okay."

Carter gave her an indulgent smile. "I don't mind staying a while longer. I like it up here. It's peaceful. Quiet." And he enjoyed being with her.

Emma pushed her hair away from her face and, leaning forward, wrapped her arms around her knees. "I love it up here too. I feel like I've left all the troubles and worries down there. At the ranch. Up here, it's just Adam, the horses and me trying to find the picture your Nana Beck calls The Shadow Woman."

Carter squinted across the valley, trying to find the shadow.

"The conditions have to be right…but it looks like they are today. See that rock face?" Carter pointed across the valley to the farthest mountain. "The sheer bluff above the trees to the right of that huge cleft? The shadow is on that rock face."

He shot her a quick glance, but she frowned and shook her head. So he moved a bit closer, pointing it out. As their shoulders touched, he caught a hint of almonds blended with the faintest scent of leather. Her hair, lifted by the wind, tickled his cheek.

He dragged his attention back to the shadow. "See those two dark holes? Those are two caves, her eyes. The rock jutting out makes her nose."

He looked over at her again and now they were side by side, but she was still frowning. "That long shadow—

that's her hair, and then below the caves—" He leaned a bit closer, following the shadow with his forefinger, pointing it out.

"Oh. Of course. I see it now. I see it." Emma clapped her hands in a girlish gesture. "And that's her dress. The one that the man in the legend bought her."

"The man she is waiting for," Carter added.

Emma grinned, looking well satisfied with herself. "I finally found it. I've been looking since I came here."

"Like I said the conditions have to be exactly right. She's easier to see in the summer and up here, easier yet." Carter smiled. "I used to feel sorry for her, forever waiting for her love to come back."

"I'm glad that your family story has a happier ending." Emma smiled and leaned back against the tree. "Though I think your Nana feels like her story won't have a happy ending until all of her grandchildren are back. Even Shannon talks about moving away, after Arthur called off the wedding."

"It's been tough on her. Shannon told me every time she had to cancel some part of the wedding, she felt ashamed again." Carter blew out a sigh, feeling a flash of sympathy for his cousin.

"I know exactly how she feels," Emma said quietly, twisting a blade of grass around her fingers as she looked at the shadow on the mountain. "It's not easy finding out that someone you trusted wasn't worthy of that trust." But before he could comment on that, she gave a light laugh. "What about the rest of the kids? Hailey, Garret, Naomi? Do you think any of them will come back again?"

Carter pursed his lips, thinking. "I know Hailey was thinking of coming back after Nana's heart attack. To be around Nana for a while. Naomi hasn't been able to get here yet and is feeling horrible about that. When Garret came to see Nana in the hospital, he talked about coming back to Hartley Creek for good. But we'll see."

"And you're moving." Then she waved her hand, as if to erase what she had just said. "I'm sorry, I didn't mean to make you feel guilty about your plans."

Carter paused, looking at Emma, then took a chance. "If I follow through on them."

Emma's eyes widened. Then she looked down, as if afraid to let Carter see what she was thinking. "What... what do you mean?" she asked, her voice quiet.

"I don't know what I want anymore." The words spilled out before he could stop them.

Emma's eyes sprang to his. "What are you saying?" she asked as he moved nearer.

Then they were face-to-face, so close that their breaths mingled.

A strand of hair stuck against her mouth. Carter reached up to brush it away the same time Emma did. Their hands met, and before he realized what he was doing, Carter caught her hand in his.

He saw her swallow, look down. But she didn't let go. Nor did she move away.

The silence surrounded them, creating a bubble of solitude. Maybe it was loneliness, maybe it was the attraction Carter felt brewing between them. Maybe it was more than that.

He dismissed his thoughts, leaned closer and their lips met. Touched. Withdrew. Then met again.

Then his arms were around her, holding her close. Hers were around him, one hand clutching the back of his neck, the other pressing against his back.

She tasted like cookie. Like sweetness. Like Emma.

He knew he should stop, yet it felt so right. As if it was the right step in the right direction.

For the first time in years, Carter Beck felt as if he had truly come home.

Chapter Ten

Pull away. Now. Stop this before you lose yourself.

Emma let her one hand drift away from Carter's neck to his shoulder. She gave a gentle, halfhearted push, and when Carter drew back, she felt bereft in spite of her self-talk.

Then she looked up at him, lost herself in his eyes, and this time she was the one who leaned in. Her lips brushed across his, generating a yearning that could be satisfied only with another kiss. With being held close to him.

Adam murmured, and like a splash of cold water, his presence intruded into the moment.

She pulled away, pressing her hands to her heated cheeks. What was she doing?

"I'm sorry," she muttered. "I shouldn't have let this happen."

Carter put his hand under her chin and turned her face up to his. "You didn't 'let' this happen," he said. "I started it."

"I know, but I let you…and I shouldn't…"

She wanted to look away, but his hand still held her chin and, if she were honest, her protests were more symbolic than anything.

The past few days with Carter had been a mixture of emotions and feelings she couldn't sort out. This kiss they shared only added to her confusion.

Then his vague comment about not knowing what he wanted? It raised a hope in her she didn't dare latch onto.

Carter's fingers caressed her cheek, but then, thankfully, he lowered his hand.

"Traditionally, this is where the guy apologizes for the kiss, but the only thing I should feel sorry about is that I'm not sorry." A crooked grin followed this admission, and Emma felt her feeble resistance shift.

Emma glanced from him back to Adam, reminding herself of her priority.

"He's still sleeping," Carter said.

"It's not that." She looked down at her hands with their broken nails, her mind casting about for the right way to express her reasons. "Adam depends on me to take care of him and to provide for him. I'm the only person in his life. He doesn't have aunts or uncles or cousins or grandparents. It's only me. And I have to make sure that all my decisions are what's best for him."

Carter said nothing to that, and Emma kept her gaze on her hands, her heart thrumming in her chest with a mixture of anticipation and concern. "Right now your plans are to sell the ranch and leave."

"What if I tell you that things might change? What if I tell you that I might—"

"Mom? Where are you?"

Adam's plaintive voice cut into what he was going to say, the reality of his presence underlining what she had told Carter.

Emma jumped to her feet and ran to Adam's side. He was sitting up, stretching his arms, and when he saw her he grinned. "Did you eat all the cookies?"

"No, honey. There are lots left." Emma went to grab the bag, but when she did, she was disappointed to see her hands trembling. She balled her hands into fists and tried again. "Here you go, buddy," she said, giving him a cookie. She set the bag aside and pulled him onto her lap, holding him close as she always did after his nap.

Focus. Adam is the nucleus of your life. He depends completely on every decision you make. Don't get distracted.

Even as she formulated that thought, she shot a quick glance toward Carter who was watching her and Adam. His "what-ifs" rang through her mind, bringing more confusion.

And she knew that Carter was becoming more than a distraction. He was becoming intertwined in her and Adam's lives.

Carter and his horse topped the rise, and then below him lay the ranch buildings.

Behind him he heard the plop of Emma's and Adam's horses' hooves on the trail still wet from the rains of the past few days, the jingle of their bridles, the squeak of the saddles as they shifted with their horses' movements.

Even more than that, it was as if he felt them behind him. Felt their very presence.

He tugged on the brim of his hat and blew out a breath. What had he done back there? What had he started?

He resisted the urge to look back over his shoulder, to catch Emma's eye. Ever since the kiss, she had avoided looking at him. As if she regretted their moment of intimacy.

He guided Banjo down the trail, easing up on the reins as he slipped then caught his footing.

All the way back from the picnic, Emma said nothing.

Adam, seemingly oblivious to the tension between Emma and Carter had chatted about the weather, the horses. How his mom said he could ride in the tractor with Wade when he cut the hay and wondering how many bales they might get.

Each comment about the ranch hit like a tiny lash. Carter doubted that Emma and Adam would be around when haying time came. He understood from Pete that the buyer was anxious, well financed and ready to take over the ranch very soon.

The thought he had tentatively expressed to Emma blew back into his mind. What if he didn't sell the place? What if he decided he wanted to come back here? Start ranching again?

With Emma and Adam?

Carter shot a glance back at Emma, and in that moment she looked over at him. Then a flush colored her cheeks and she looked away. What was she thinking?

When they got back to the ranch, he knew they needed to talk more. She needed to know that his kiss wasn't simply a casual thing. And he wanted—no, needed—to know her reaction. He didn't dare build a potential future on such a flimsy foundation as a kiss.

She's pretty. You kissed. What does it matter?

The trouble was, it did.

Emma was more than an attractive woman. She was a mother with a mother's responsibilities. He had to take Adam's needs into consideration as, he was sure, Emma did. Could he take on this little boy, as well? He couldn't make that decision lightly.

He glanced over at Adam, who grinned back at him, and Carter felt that warmth again. That sense of connection. Then his gaze drifted to Emma, who was watching him with puzzlement in her expression.

He squared his shoulders then turned, looking at the ranch buildings as they came closer. He and his grandfather had put up the hay shed, the shop and the small garage by the house. His great-grandfather had built the barn and the corrals and the house he had lived in.

With every step of Banjo's hooves toward the ranch, history pulled at him. Memories slipped into his mind. Naomi and Shannon screaming as Garret and Carter dumped them into the river. Hailey trying to snowboard off the roof of the hay shed and breaking her leg.

Papa Beck taking them on a wagon ride every year after haying was done. The wagon ride was one of the highlights of the year for the cousins. That, and Christmas when everyone came together at the ranch, singing carols with Papa and Nana Beck, unwrapping presents, eating way too many cinnamon buns.

The memories rolled over one another, braided snatches of voices, songs. Good memories folding over the sad ones.

Did he have to sell this place? Did he have to leave?

Peace is not the absence of trouble, peace is the presence of God.

He turned Banjo's head to make the last turn down the hill to the ranch as he thought again what the pastor had said on Sunday.

Dear God, he prayed, struggling to find the right words to address someone he hadn't talked to in a long while. *I don't know what to think. Show me what to do.*

Behind that prayer came a measure of peace. A sense of wait-and-see. He had time yet. He didn't have to make a decision today. Or tomorrow.

He and Emma could explore where things were going. He wanted to spend more time with Adam, too. To find a place for the boy in his life. If, indeed, that was the direction he and Emma would go.

"Who is visiting Nana Beck?"

Adam's voice startled him out of his thoughts. Adam was pointing at Nana's house, and Emma's attention was on Adam.

Tonight, he thought, tonight he wanted to talk to her.

He turned back to the house, and from here he saw the two figures Adam had referred to, sitting on the deck of his grandmother's house. Probably someone from church.

He reined his horse right, toward the corrals, and rode past the pasture. Banjo whinnied and the other horses called back then ran to join them.

"Yeah, yeah, I'm sure you missed these guys horribly," Carter said as he dismounted by the hitching rail.

To his surprise, he wasn't near as stiff as before. Getting used to riding again, he thought with a satisfied smile while looping the reins over Banjo's head.

"Those people are coming over here," Adam was saying as Emma helped him off the saddle.

The man walking toward them was tall, thin, with close-cropped graying hair and a net of wrinkles around his deep-blue eyes. His suit coat hung loose on his narrow shoulders, and his blue jeans were crisp and new over his cowboy boots.

The woman was short, plump, with curly hair framing her face. She wore a long skirt, a T-shirt and flip-flops.

As Sylvia always did.

"Do you know who they are?" Emma asked, glancing sidelong at Carter.

Carter's heart slowed, then began racing.

"Yeah. Those are Sylvia's parents. Harry's grandparents." His voice choked on the last sentence.

What were they doing here? How come they didn't

tell him they were coming? What was he supposed to do with them?

"I'll take care of Banjo," Emma said quietly, coming to stand beside him.

He glanced down at her, then back at Sylvia's parents. The last time he saw them was across Harry's grave. After the agonizing reception in the church, he had raced home, thrown his things together, given Wade a few muttered instructions with promises for more to come later, hopped on his motorbike and left. He hadn't seen them since.

Carter dragged his attention back to Emma, his emotions a whirlwind of confusion, guilt and yet…his heart softened a moment as his eyes met hers.

Too easily he recalled what it was like to hold her in his arms. That feeling of everything being right in his world, if only for a moment.

"That's…that's okay. I'll deal with it."

"I'm sure you'll want to talk to them." Emma reached over and took Banjo's reins. "I know they want to talk to you. Very badly."

Carter held on to the reins, catching her attention. "The only person I want to talk to right now is you."

She blinked, but then her eyes lowered. "I don't know… I'm not sure."

"Neither am I," he said, an urgency entering his voice as he heard Kim Groot calling his name. "But what happened up there was more than just a kiss. You and I both know that."

She shot him a quick look, and in her eyes he caught a hint of uncertainty, which gave him hope. "Maybe, but right now you have other things to deal with."

"Later, then. We'll talk later."

She gave him a shy smile, a quick nod, and then before

he could say anything more, the past caught up to the present.

"Carter." Kim Groot's voice fluttered across the moment and then Kim enveloped him in an awkward hug, her tears wetting his shirt.

He lifted his free hand and patted her on the shoulder, unsure of what was expected of him. Over Kim's head he saw Sylvia's father, Frank, reach up and swipe a hand over his eyes.

Emma eased away from him, leading Banjo, Dusty and Diamond to the pasture.

"Oh, son, it has been too long," Kim was saying as she stepped back and wiped away the moisture running down her cheeks. She looked up at him, her green eyes, so much like Sylvia's, red and glistening with tears.

Frank moved closer, laying his hand on Carter's shoulder. "Sorry for dropping in on you like this, but we haven't talked to you. Haven't seen you since—" His voice broke again, and Carter felt slowly drawn back to a storm of emotions he had tried to avoid for the past two years.

"Since the funeral," he said quietly, surprised at how calm and even his voice sounded.

Frank nodded, drawing in a shaky breath. He pulled a worn hanky out of his pocket and handed it to Kim. She wiped her eyes, blew her nose and gave Carter a wavery smile.

"Like Frank said, I'm sorry for doing this to you, but I did call. Some girl answered."

"Emma," Carter said. "That's Emma who was here a moment ago." Emma who was now putting the horses away in the corral. Emma whom he had just kissed. Emma who was confusing him more than he had ever been confused before.

"Who is the little boy?"

As Carter dragged his attention away from Emma, he caught a peculiar inflection in Kim's voice and a frown on her face. Carter recognized the emotion. He had felt the same way when he first saw Adam on the ranch.

As if the child was an interloper.

"That's Adam. Her son."

"So she's married?"

"No."

Kim nodded slowly, as if pondering this situation. Carter wasn't sure what to make of her frown or the way her lips were pressed together. He wanted to defend Emma. To explain what she was really like.

"She seems to know how to handle horses," Frank said.

"She's good with them. And she loves the ranch."

"Sylvia loved the ranch so much," Kim said, a defensive note in her voice. "And I know she loved riding."

Frank frowned. "What do you mean? Sylvia was uncomfortable around the horses."

"No, she wasn't, was she, Carter?"

Carter's mind raced, trying to find a diplomatic way to answer his mother-in-law. Sylvia was an amazing woman and a wonderful wife, but she went riding with him only once or twice.

"How are you doing, Carter?" Frank asked, thankfully rescuing him from answering.

"I'm doing okay," he said quietly, shoving his gloves in his back pocket.

"We missed you, son," Frank said, his voice gentle. "It's been a long hard road for us, and we wanted to talk to you once in a while. Just to see how you were doing."

"But we couldn't because you were gone," Kim added, curving her arm through her husband's. "You're the only connection that remains to Harry and Sylvia. You're all we have left of our grandson and beautiful daughter." She sniffed and drew in a long breath. "She was so precious to us. She's been gone five years, but at times I still expect to see her coming through the door of our house singing those hymns she loved. She was such an example to me, so strong in her faith. I still don't understand why God took her away from us."

Carter didn't either, but he found he didn't want to talk about Sylvia. Not out here. Not in front of Emma.

"And then to lose Harry." Kim reached over and laid her hand on his arm. "If we feel the loss so keenly, you must feel it even more."

Each word Kim spoke laid another brick of guilt on his shoulders. The guilt of a man who couldn't keep his wife from dying. Who couldn't keep his son safe.

He thought about the kiss he and Emma shared. The feeling that overwhelmed him when he held her in his arms. He hadn't felt that way in so long.

But Kim's words haunted him.

How could he consider taking care of Emma or Adam?

Chapter Eleven

So what was she supposed to do? Sit and wait for Carter to come to her? Go to him?

Emma fidgeted in the easy chair tucked in one corner of her and Adam's cabin, her book forgotten on her lap. Adam snored lightly in his bed, the fresh air and excitement catching up to him.

Carter's in-laws had left over an hour ago. But still Carter didn't come. He had said he needed to talk to her. So where was he? Had seeing Sylvia's parents reminded him of his past too much, putting any future plans in jeopardy?

She rubbed her forehead, pressing away a headache that threatened. Too many thoughts roiling through her head. Too much to figure out. At one time she had a plan. A purpose. A goal.

Now she felt as if her life had been tossed upside down. As if God was playing some joke on her.

And Carter was becoming…what? Important to her? Special?

Her fingers drifted to her lips as if trying to find the kiss she had given him.

Oh, Emma, you are such a silly fool. Didn't you learn your lesson with Karl? With Adam's father?

But in the deepest places of her heart she sensed Carter was different. The fact that he grieved for his son, grieved for his wife, though hard to watch, showed her that relationships were important to him. He wouldn't have kissed her if he didn't mean it. Wouldn't have treated that lightly.

He's a guy. You know you can't depend on them. Where is he now? He said he wanted to talk to you, but where is he?

Emma tossed her book aside and reached for her Bible, hoping to find solace there. But as she turned the pages, the words blurred into each other.

She wanted to draw nourishment from scripture, but her mind kept slipping to what she and Carter had shared this afternoon.

Then a knock on the door sent her heart into overdrive.

She waited a moment, sent up a prayer for strength and opened the door of the cabin. Carter stood there on her deck, the light behind him casting shadows on his face. She couldn't read his expression.

She glanced back at Adam then stepped outside and closed the door, shutting off the light coming from the cabin. Carter became a darkened outline against the remnants of daylight.

"What do you want?" she asked, struggling and failing to sound in control.

Carter blew out a sigh and shoved one hand through his hair. "I want to talk to you."

Emma's heart fluttered at his admission, but the hoarse sound of his voice sent a chill of foreboding, chasing the momentary excitement away.

"Can we sit down?" he asked, walking over to a wooden bench.

Emma hesitated, then perched on the side of the bench closest to the window so she could watch Adam and be reminded of her first responsibility.

Carter eased himself down beside her.

He leaned forward, his elbows resting on his knees, his hands clasped between his legs,

"So, how were Kim and Frank Groot?" she asked, determined to be in charge of the conversation.

Carter pinched the bridge of his nose with his thumb and forefinger, kneading it slowly. "When you told me I should talk to them, I had hoped it would be on my time." He released a sigh into the gathering dark. "It was hard seeing them." Carter's voice faltered, and Emma felt a surge of pity for him as quiet fell between them again. This time Emma said nothing and waited for him to bridge the gap his silence had created.

"Did anyone tell you how Harry died?" Carter asked.

Emma shook her head. Wade had only said that Harry had died on the ranch. Nana Beck didn't tell her much more than that, and Emma hadn't pried.

"Remember how you commented on the fact that I didn't have a horse waterer on the place?"

She simply nodded.

"I had one once. A big plastic tub. The kind you attach a hose to and a switch shuts the hose off when the water level gets high enough."

"My dad had a couple of them on the yard." She wasn't crazy about them, but they were cheaper than putting in an underground heated waterer.

Carter dragged his hand over his face then exhaled slowly. "Wade and I had to go up to the high pasture and gather up some stray cows. Nana Beck usually babysat Harry, but she had the flu so I got someone to come in. She was an older woman who used to live down the road.

She fell asleep on the couch. My son…Harry wasn't even in bed yet. He walked out of the house and went over to the corral to look at the horses. Probably feed them some carrots." He gave a short laugh. "He used to do that all the time. I noticed Adam does too."

Silence followed his comment, and Emma waited.

He drew in a shaky breath. "No one knows what happened. Whether he hit his head, or fell or one of the horses scared him. Wade came on the yard first and found him facedown in the waterer." He stopped there, staring straight ahead.

The heaviness of his words fell between them, creating a chasm she didn't know how to bridge with words. Finally, she realized nothing she said would make a difference. So she took his cold hands and wrapped hers around them.

His fingers tightened as he drew in a ragged breath. He clung to her hand, then turned it over in his grasp. "I should have been here. I should have stayed home. Should have let Wade take care of the cows himself. Harry was my responsibility, and I should have been here to…to save him."

His voice broke, and it was that mournful sound that eased away the flimsy barriers she tried to erect against him.

She cupped his chin in her hand and turned his face to her. "It was an accident."

"But he was my son. He counted on me to take care of him. I promised Sylvia I would take care of him."

"How were you supposed to stop what happened?"

He said nothing, but in the light of the cabin she caught the sheen of tears in his eyes.

"You took care of him. You got someone to come and

watch him. What happened was a tragedy. An accident you couldn't have prevented."

Carter's eyes drifted shut and his tears slid down his cheeks, flowing over Emma's hand. "He was my son. My son." The words were ripped from the deepest part of him.

Emma slid her arms around his shoulders, wishing she was stronger, bigger. How could she help him in his grief when her arms barely went around him? How could she support him when he towered over her?

Then Carter laid his head on her shoulder, his arms clinging to her. And as his silent tears flowed, she knew all she had to do was be here. His shoulders shook and she held him, realizing his tears were cleansing, as well.

Seeing this strong, self-assured man crying brought tears to her own eyes. Yet, his utter vulnerability dove into her soul. His tears, shed in front of her, were as intimate as the kiss they had shared. Nothing would be the same between them after today.

"It's okay," she murmured, holding him as tightly as she could, thankful she could be here for him. "It's okay."

He drew a deep breath, then slowly straightened, leaving her feeling incomplete. He palmed away his tears, removing the evidence of his weakness.

He couldn't look at her, but she kept her hand on his shoulder and caught his other hand in hers.

"I'm sorry," he whispered, his voice still hoarse with grief. "I don't know what happened there. I haven't cried since the funeral."

She stroked his unruly hair back from his forehead. "That's probably why," she said, her voice quiet, her hand lingering a moment on his head.

"But it's been two years." His voice held an edge of

disappointed anger, as if frustrated with his lack of self-control. "Why now?"

She cupped his face and turned it toward her. His eyes, red now, looked haunted, but in contrast the lines bracketing his mouth had softened. "Could it be because you didn't allow your family to enter in your grief?"

Carter's shoulders lifted as he breathed in. Then he exhaled slowly, as if expelling the grief he had just experienced.

"I couldn't face it. I couldn't think about it, let alone talk about it. I lost Sylvia and then I lost Harry. It seemed easier to shut the memories off. To push them down and bury them. To pull back from my family."

"When you do that, grief will have its way," Emma said quietly, reluctantly pulling her hand away, his whiskers rasping on her skin. "After my father died, I was so angry with him but I still missed him so badly. At first I didn't want to cry, but the tears came anyhow. It's as if grief requires a certain amount of tears. If they are not shed, grief follows and shadows us until it is paid its due."

Carter gave a short laugh. "It certainly followed and shadowed me." His fingers pressed tightly against hers, as if drawing strength from her.

"Now that you're back I'm sure the pain is back."

His only response was a nod and a tightening of his jaw.

"Maybe seeing Sylvia's parents—Harry's grandparents—triggered the sorrow?"

Carter drew in another breath then his mouth lifted in a wry smile. "Maybe. We talked and I realized it was like you said. They wanted to share stories. To talk."

"Was that difficult?"

"At first, yeah. I thought I didn't want to talk about him ever again. And yet..." His words drifted off and then, to her surprise, his mouth curved in a wry smile. "It hurt and it was hard to watch their grief, but at the same time, it was like I was allowed to still say he was my son. I was allowed to bring back the good memories. The things that made me smile and gave me joy."

"Why wouldn't you?"

Carter lifted his shoulder in a shrug. "Because I didn't think I deserved to."

"I know you were a good father, Carter." Emma spoke quietly, a note of conviction in her voice. "You loved your son. Your tears showed me that. Even the fact that you stayed away because it hurt to be here shows how much you love and miss him." She had to stop, her own thoughts casting back to Adam's father. How quickly he neglected his responsibility. Or Karl. How easily he abandoned her. Or her father.

Panic trembled through her even as his hands held hers. Carter wasn't like that, she reminded herself. Carter was a good man.

Why do you think you need to defend him? I thought you were trying to stay away from him?

"You took care of your son even while you were still running the ranch," she said, trying to stop the negative voice in her head. "You manned up. You took your responsibility seriously and you took care of him. And even though you knew it would hurt to be here again, you came back when Nana needed you."

He looked down at her, his gray eyes clear, intent. "You sound like you're defending me."

"Maybe I am," she said quietly. "Maybe I need to remind myself that there are good men in the world."

"I don't know if I'm a good man…" Carter's words eased away and his grip tightened on her hand. "But I know that you're a good woman."

His words flew into her heart and settled there.

And confused her. She struggled to keep a bit of distance. She couldn't get pulled into this.

"I know that God knows your heart in spite of how you see yourself," she said quietly.

"I used to think God didn't care about me," Carter said. "I used to think I was on my own."

"And now?"

Carter released a light laugh. "I don't know. I know that when I was in church I fought with anger with God over what happened and yet..." He shook his head, as if confused.

"Yet?" she prompted.

"It was good to realize that God is still there no matter what I may think. That He is still trying to be a part of my life. I feel like I have to try to find my way back to Him."

"It's not hard," Emma said quietly.

"I don't know where to start."

"I could pray with you. That would be a start."

Carter's mouth shifted into a wry smile. "You could," he agreed.

Emma twined her fingers through his then lowered her head. "Dear Lord, thank You for Carter. For his doubts and for his anger with You. Because it means that he cares about You. Lord, You know the pain he's carrying. Please let him know that You understand what it is like to lose a son." She faltered there, wondering if she had gone too far, then she felt Carter's hands tighten on hers and she carried on. "Thank You, Lord, for his searching. Let him know that he will be restless until he finds his rest in You. Help all of us to know where our hope and peace lie. With You. Not with this world." She paused, letting the moment settle. Then she lifted her head.

Carter was looking at her, a bemused expression on his face. "You talk so easily to God," he said.

"I didn't always. I've had my own struggles with God and with my life and the direction it was going." She looked down at their intertwined hands, feeling as if things had shifted again. Shifted and deepened. "But I learned that no matter where I go, God has been there before and He promises me that He will never leave me. I've clung to that promise in spite of some of the things that happened to me." She stopped there, hoping he didn't think she was preaching at him, yet wanting him to know that her faith in God was not dependent on her actions, but on God's faithfulness. And His love.

"You're quite a woman, Emma Minton," Carter said quietly, lifting his hand to cup her face. "Thank you for praying with me."

She wasn't sure what to say so she kept quiet, but the touch of his hand on her face distracted her.

Then his thumb made gentle circles on her cheek, each movement shifting her awareness of him.

"I'm glad I kissed you this afternoon." His hand stopped its enticing movement then slipped to the back of her neck and anchored itself there.

"I'm glad you kissed me too." She raised her face, their gazes locking. She felt as if she sank into his eyes.

"I want to kiss you again," he whispered.

The practical part of Emma called out warnings. Reminded her that this was tenuous. That nothing about either of their lives was settled or sure.

But the lonely part of her, the part that yearned for what Carter gave, made her move closer. She set her hand on his shoulder then angled her head so that when their lips met, it was a perfect fit.

He pulled away and she murmured her protest, but he

brushed light, gentle kisses on her cheeks. Her forehead. Her eyelids.

She couldn't breathe. His kisses had literally stolen her breath.

Then he drew her head down to his shoulder, cradling it there and pulling her close to him.

Emma let her head rest on his shoulder. Let his arms hold her close. Let herself be held up. She had been in charge of her and Adam so long, having someone support her filled a deep need she didn't dare acknowledge.

"I don't know what's happening, Emma," Carter whispered against her hair, his breath warm and enticing. "But I know it feels right. Like my life has turned around and the things I once wanted aren't so important."

His questions ignited an ember of hope.

But her own questions and concerns kept it tamped down. Tomorrow would bring more questions. More searching. More maybes.

For now the chill of the evening made itself known. Emma shivered and eased away from the sanctuary of Carter's arms. "I should go in," she whispered, her cheeks warm in spite of the cold. She looked up at him, then, because she could, stroked his face and ran her hand through his thick hair.

He caught her hand, pressed a kiss to the back of it. "I'll see you tomorrow."

The promise in his voice sent a thrill of anticipation racing through her.

"It's Sunday tomorrow," she said quietly, though she wasn't sure why she felt she had to bring that up.

"Do you need a ride to church? I'm bringing Nana in her car."

His suggestion created such a perfect domestic scene in

her mind. Man. Woman. Child. Grandmother. All coming
to church together in one vehicle.

In spite of his kisses, in spite of what they had shared,
a part of her wanted to hold back and protect her inde-
pendence. Just in case.

"I'll take my truck," was all she said.

To her surprise he simply nodded as he got up, drawing her to her feet. "Then we'll see you tomorrow."

He walked with her the few steps to the door of the
cabin. "Good night Emma. Thank you for being you," he
whispered as he brushed a kiss across her forehead.

Then before his kiss cooled on her face, he was down
the stairs, jogging across the yard to his own cabin.

Emma waited a moment, unwilling to return to the
cabin. This time was like a place apart from her ordinary
life. As soon as she opened the door, she would be faced
with her responsibilities.

Just a few minutes more, she thought, her finger trac-
ing her lips, resurrecting the memory of Carter's kiss.

Tomorrow she could figure out where to put this. Tomorrow she could be a responsible mom again. Tomorrow her other worries would crowd in and threaten this
peace.

For this moment she wanted to be a woman kissed by
a wonderful man. A woman growing more attracted to a
man with nebulous plans.

She stopped herself there.

A tendril of worry began working itself up from her
subconscious. Was she being irresponsible? She had no
idea what lay ahead, and Carter's comments were nothing to make plans around.

*Do not worry about tomorrow for tomorrow will worry
about itself.*

The passage from Matthew settled her thoughts, and

as she looked up a falling star streaked across the evening sky, like a tiny benediction. Emma smiled at the sight, and with that memory resting in her mind, she opened the door and stepped into the cabin.

"Miss Minton. Miss Minton."

Emma pulled her attention away from the woman she was talking to in the foyer of the church and turned just as a slight man limped toward her. The overhead lights shone on his balding head, which was offset by the bushiness of his beard and mustache.

"Mr. Devieber, how are you doing?" Emma flashed him a bright smile as he came to a halt in front of her. Scott Devieber owned a bed-and-breakfast on the edge of Hartley Creek, and on a whim she had gone there and applied for a position the last time she was in town. The biggest plus was the fact that the B and B was situated on six acres of fenced pasture. "How is business?"

Scott stroked his beard as he nodded his head. "Well. Now. That's what I need to talk to you about." He eased out a sigh, shifted his weight, neither of which boded well for what she supposed he had to say. "I had hoped to call you earlier, but because you don't have a cell phone, I gotta tell you now." His pause only underlined what Emma knew was coming next. "Sorry, Emma. I'm sure you're a great worker, but I can't hire you."

And you had to tell me this on Sunday right after a service where I was encouraged to trust in the Lord?

With intense purpose, Emma kept her smile in place. "That's too bad, Mr. Devieber. Did you fill the position?" When she had applied it was vacant, and in a follow-up phone call Mr. Devieber assured her that she had a good chance at the job.

"Actually, I have a niece coming to visit me from New

Zealand. She's looking for work. Says she wants to spend the winter skiing here." He lifted his hands in a "what can I do" gesture.

"Of course. I understand," Emma said brightly, though inside another hope died. Another worry twisted its way through the peace the church service had granted her.

What was she supposed to do? How was she going to take care of Adam? Where were they going to live, and what was she going to do with her beloved horses?

"But I trust in you O Lord; I say, 'You are my God.' My times are in your hands..."

The words of the Bible verse the minister had read this morning wound their way around her panicky soul.

"I hope she enjoys her time here," Emma said, struggling to be upbeat and positive. "I know that the ski hill is amazing." Not that she knew from personal experience. She hadn't had the time or money to go skiing.

"I'm sorry. I know this position would have worked well for you and your horses. But I'm sure you'll find something." He stroked his beard, gave her another apologetic look then left.

Scratch that faint hope, Emma thought. She turned in time to see Adam slouching toward her, his head down, his hands shoved in the pocket of his red hoodie.

"What's the matter, son?" she asked, crouching down to his height, no mean feat in her narrow skirt. "You look sad."

"Allister can't come over," he said, heaving a deep sigh. "I wanted him to help with the tree fort. I'm so disappointed."

In spite of her own disappointments, Emma grinned at his word choice. He was getting older, she thought with a gentle pang. This September he would be starting school. Where? How?

Emma quashed the frantic questions.

"I'm disappointed too," Emma said, stroking his head lightly. "But you know, maybe you and I can work on the tree fort ourselves."

Adam shrugged at her suggestion.

"What? I'm a good builder," she said with mock injury.

Adam pushed his toe against the carpet of the church foyer. "Not as good as Allister. He has a hammer."

"Who has a hammer?"

Carter's deep voice behind her created a trickle of anticipation.

She got up slowly, unconsciously fiddling with the white silk flower she had, on a whim, pinned on her red blouse. Now it seemed ostentatious and a little foolish.

She caught his gaze flicking from the flower to her. Did his eyes brighten, or was that just her imagination?

"Allister. My friend," Adam grumped. "He was going to help me with the tree fort. But now he can't come." This was followed with another theatrical sigh.

Carter turned his attention to Adam, and he smiled, as well. "Maybe I'll have to help you."

Emma hoped her surprise didn't show on her face. She knew Carter and Harry had started the tree fort, and now he was willing to help her son work on it?

"That would be so, so cool." Adam's face lit up like a kid at Christmas.

"Don't you need to cut the hay this week?" Emma asked.

"Yeah, but I'm sure I can take some time to help Adam." Carter's eyes crinkled at the corners as their gazes met, and a smile crawled across his lips.

Emma felt her own answering smile, and it was as if the people milling around them in the foyer slipped away and the world had shrunk down to only the two of them.

"That would be great," she said quietly.

Emma wanted to ask him if he was okay working on a project he had started with Harry, but now was not the time. Maybe later.

Later. The possibilities of that word created a tiny thrill of expectation.

"So, my dears, what are you all doing for lunch?" Nana Beck joined them, her bright eyes flicking around the group.

Emma caught a gleam in the elderly woman's eye as she zeroed in on Emma and Carter. *Don't blush. Don't blush.*

But the more aware she became of her reaction, the harder it became to suppress.

And the gleam in Nana Beck's eyes grew.

"Shannon wants us to come for dinner," Nana announced. "And don't you even think about protesting, Emma Minton. You and Adam are invited too." She leveled Emma a glance that brooked no argument. Before Emma could either accept or decline, an older woman tugged on Nana's arm, drawing her attention away from Emma and Carter.

"Sorry about that," Carter was saying. "But you know Nana. If you want to go home, that's okay."

Emma was thankful for the out he gave her, yet some ornery part of her wished he insisted she come.

Then he moved a bit closer and brushed his hand along her arm. "But I'd kind of like it if you did come."

That was all the encouragement she needed.

"Are you sure you want the door here?" Carter called out.

Emma shaded her face against the lowering sun and

looked up at Carter standing astride the uprights of the tree fort, shadows of branches crisscrossing over his shirt.

"That looks good to me," she called out. "What do you think, Adam?"

Adam squinted up at Carter, his hand on his hips, looking like a little adult as he considered. "I think so," he said with a quick nod.

"Starting to saw," Carter announced, yanking on the starting cord of the chain saw. Chips of wood spat out as the saw bit into the solid wall of the fort, and minutes later Carter had cut an opening.

"Are you guys almost done here?" Emma asked Adam. "It's your bedtime."

"Can't I stay up a bit longer?" Adam whined. "I want to finish making the door."

"That's not going to happen tonight, sport." Carter lowered the chain saw by a rope then clambered down the ladder he had built last night. For the past three days Carter had worked in the evenings, helping Adam as he had promised. And each day his smile grew bigger and Adam's anticipation ran higher.

And the tiny spark of hope ignited that night on the porch with Carter grew in Emma's chest. Carter had never said anything more about his plans, but she got the sense that both of them were hovering on the edge of a change. A shift in direction.

Once down on the ground, Carter looked up at the sky and the gathering clouds. "Glad we got that hay cut today," he said. "Looks like rain's coming." He gave her a quick smile then, as casual as can be, he ran his forefinger down her cheek.

His offhand familiarity formed a mixture of perplexing emotions.

The past week with Carter was time out of time. A step

back from her world of worry and concern and fear for the future. It was as if she and Carter had an unspoken pact to see where they were going without talking about it.

They worked together and ate together at Nana Beck's in the evening. After dinner they sat around and visited. After Adam went to bed, Carter would come by and he and Emma would sit on the deck and talk.

They talked about the ranch. About Sylvia. And even about Harry once in a while. Carter's voice still held a trace of pain when they did, but each time Harry's name came up, Carter seemed more at peace.

And each time they talked, Emma let herself experience the potential of possibilities. Of hesitant maybes.

"I hope it doesn't rain too long," Emma said, struggling to keep herself grounded. "I want to get some more beans picked this week."

"Nana sure appreciates the fresh produce," Carter said. "And she enjoys our dinners together."

Emma looked up at him. "I do too. Nana is a special person. I'm glad she's feeling better. Do you think she'll change her mind about moving into town?"

"I don't think so." Carter's expression grew serious, and he caught one corner of his lip between his teeth. "And about that. I need to talk to you later," he said, his voice holding a curious note.

"Sure. Of course." She felt puzzled at his sudden switch in topic, but the intensity of his expression and the way he held her gaze sent a storm of worry swirling through her head. They'd been talking for the past few evenings. What could he say to her tonight that he hadn't said in previous nights?

"Looking forward to it," she said, keeping her tone light. Playful.

He just looked at her, and the storm grew.

Then he picked up the chain saw and walked toward the machine shed.

"Mom, do I have to go to bed? Can I work a bit more?" Adam picked up a hammer and a handful of nails.

Emma snapped her attention back to her son. "No, son, tomorrow is another day."

"But…"

"No buts. You need to go to bed. Now let's put the tools away."

"I don't want to go to bed." Adam's lower lip quivered, which showed Emma that bed was not an option, it was a necessity.

"Of course you don't." Emma gently removed the hammer from his hand. "It's hard to go to bed when there's so many fun things to do."

"Tomorrow can we go up to the hills to get the lanterns out of the cabin? For my fort?"

"No. I don't think so."

"But in a couple of days Carter will be gone, and I want him to finish the tree fort before he goes."

"What?" Emma felt her heart slow and turn over. "What do you mean Carter will be gone?"

"I heard him say to Nana that he had to go. So we have to get the stuff tomorrow. *Have to.* So we can finish before he goes." Adam tugged on her hand as if for emphasis.

Emma swallowed as her heart raced in her chest. Her cheeks burned as reaction set in. Carter. Saying he had to leave?

This didn't ring true with Carter's current behavior. *Men can't be trusted. Men can't be trusted.*

The old voice returned and, with it, her usual doubts. But he had kissed her. He talked about making changes. He wanted to speak to her tonight. Surely it wasn't to tell her he was leaving? Not after what they had shared?

"That's why I want to finish the fort," Adam was saying, his voice taking on a petulant whine. "And go get the stuff from the cabin."

Emma dragged her attention away from the voices whirring around her head, playing on her uncertainty and the delicate balance she struggled to maintain the past few days.

"No, Adam. You have to go to bed now."

He stamped his foot in the ground, his hands clenched into little fists. "I want to go now. Right now."

"Stop it, Adam. We're not going anywhere right now. It's time for you to go to bed." She reached for his hand, but he spun away and ran toward the river. What was wrong with him?

"Adam, come back here." Her voice grew extra firm.

Adam slowed down then stopped and turned around, tears shining in his eyes. "I have to get the lantern. Because then I can put a light in the fort. So people who are lost can find it."

Her heart jolted at his little declaration. What was going through his head? Was he worried about Carter leaving?

"Adam, honey, I know you want to get the lantern. But we can't do it tonight, and we can't do it tomorrow. I promise you when we have a chance, you and I will ride up and get it."

Adam frowned at that, as if he didn't believe her. Truth to tell, she didn't blame him. She didn't know what she was allowed to think about or plan for, either.

Please, Lord. Help me to take one moment at a time.

She waited for Adam, and finally he trudged back to

her, his head hanging and his feet dragging. After half an hour of coaxing him, she tucked Adam in bed. Thankfully, he fell asleep while she said his evening prayers with him.

Emma wasn't sure what had gotten into him, but he seemed determined to get that lantern.

She waited until she knew he was well asleep, reading her Bible to still the voices of uncertainty Adam's little comment had whipped up.

Peace is not the absence of trouble, peace is the presence of God.

Emma clung to that saying and held it close. As she did, she reminded herself that her hope was primarily in God. Not in the circumstances of her life.

Adam snorted then rolled over, his arms flopping to the side. Utterly innocent, trusting and utterly dependent on her.

Emma put the Bible away, pressed a kiss to his warm cheek, then slipped out of the cabin. Usually Carter came to her cabin, but after what Adam had told her she felt restless and edgy and unable to sit still.

So instead of waiting for Carter to come to her, she would go to him.

A light rain drizzled down as she walked across the yard. Lights were on in Nana Beck's house, but Carter's cabin was dark.

As she came closer, the door of Nana's house flew open and music and noise spilled out, followed by an unfamiliar woman. "C'mon, Carter, let me check out my cabin. I can't believe you moved into it."

The woman was tall and slender, and a spill of reddish hair flowed down her back. Hailey, Emma guessed, recognizing the hair from pictures Nana Beck had shown her. Carter's cousin and Shannon's sister.

Emma held back, unsure of what to do.

She heard Shannon say something, followed by a comment from Carter. Though she couldn't understand what they said, it was apparent some type of family reunion was going on. Hailey, she knew, hadn't been around for years.

Unwilling to disturb them, she returned to her cabin. She slipped quietly inside and went to bed herself, taking her book and attaching a small reading light to it so she wouldn't wake Adam. Obviously, Carter wouldn't be talking to her tonight.

But what had he wanted to say to her?

Chapter Twelve

Emma rolled onto her side, snuggling deeper in the blankets. The only sound in the cabin was the steady drum of rain, which had poured down, hard, all night. Obviously the plans for the day would be put on hold. Which meant she and Adam could sleep a little longer.

She hoped it wouldn't cause too many problems for Carter and the hay crop.

The thought of Carter sent a tiny shock through her system.

He had said he wanted to talk to her, and though he'd had his cousins visit, she had waited for a couple of hours, clinging to a faint hope that he might come when they were gone. But when the sound of Shannon's car faded into the distance, Carter didn't come knocking on her door. When she had finally fallen asleep, it was to dream of her and Carter kissing. Her and Carter arguing. Carter driving away on his motorbike.

Emma gave up on grabbing some more sleep, sat up in bed and swung her legs over the edge, her feet looking for her slippers as she slipped her housecoat over her pajamas.

Maybe today she would find out what he wanted,

she thought, rubbing her eyes then pushing herself off the bed.

Stifling a yawn, she padded across the cold cabin floor to Adam's bed, but as she got close her heart stuttered in her chest.

Adam wasn't in his bed.

"Adam? Adam?" She tried not to let panic take root. "Adam, are you hiding?" she called out, her gaze racing around the cabin, looking for possible hiding spots.

But there was no answering giggle. No sound of a body moving anywhere in the cabin.

It took her mere seconds to plunge her legs into her jeans, stab her arms in a T-shirt and sweater. As she did, she noticed that Adam's boots were gone, as was his rain slicker.

Relax, relax, she told herself as she tugged on her boots and snatched her own slicker off the peg. Maybe he went to Nana Beck's house. Or Carter's cabin. Or the tree fort. Yes, probably the tree fort.

She grabbed her hat, slapped it on her head and ran outside.

Water poured off the roof, splashing into puddles beside the cabin as she scanned the yard, misted with rain. No sign of Adam. In the mud at the foot of the stairs she saw a set of footprints leading in the opposite direction of the tree fort, so Adam probably wasn't there. And three steps later, the footprints disappeared in the mud.

Slow down, she told herself, buttoning up her slicker, her hands numb with fear. *Don't make this bigger than it has to be. Take it one step at a time. He wouldn't have gone far.*

She jogged across the yard to Nana Beck's house and knocked on the door.

Nana came to the door, looking bright, trim and hap-

pier than Emma had seen her in a while. Then her cheer-
fulness faded into concern. "What's wrong, my dear? You
look worried."

"Have you seen Adam?" Emma asked breathlessly,
needing to get right to the point.

"Not since yesterday afternoon."

The first sliver of icy panic pierced her self-control.
"Is Carter here?"

"I believe he's in his cabin yet, though I'm surprised.
I thought for sure he would be up and about early this
morning. He said he had to get to town today. Said he had
something important to do, though he was all secretive
about it."

Part of what she said registered in Emma's mind, but
all she understood for now was that Adam wasn't here.

"Thanks, Nana. I gotta go." Emma took a step back
and spun around, clattering down the stairs, dread clenching her heart in an icy fist.

"If I see Adam, I'll tell him you're looking for him,"
Nana called out as Emma raced across the yard to Carter's
cabin.

Please, Lord, let him be there. Please Lord, she prayed
as she slipped and slid in the mud gathering on the yard.
She ran up the steps to Carter's cabin and pounded on the
door. No answer.

She raised her hand to pound again, and the door
opened.

Carter stood framed in the doorway, dressed and looking as if he was ready to go out. He wore pressed blue
jeans and an ironed khaki shirt and his motorcycle chaps
hung over his arm.

His cheeks shone from a recent shaving, and his hair
was tamed and neatly brushed.

Where was he going in this weather?

The question was banished as Emma's gaze slipped past Carter into the cabin. No little boy hove into view. No voice called out for her.

"Emma, what's wrong?" Carter tossed the chaps aside and caught her by the arms. "Your face is white as a sheet."

"Is Adam here? Have you seen him?"

Carter's grip tightened. "Not this morning. Why?"

"He's not in his bed. He's not at Nana Beck's. I didn't see him on the yard. I have no idea where he could be." She heard her voice growing more shrill and hysterical with each word, but she couldn't stop herself.

Carter's face blanched, and Emma knew exactly what he was thinking. "Okay. We need to go looking." He grabbed his slicker and hat and put them on.

"You're sure he's not at the tree fort?" Carter asked as he stepped out of the cabin.

"I saw his footprints in the mud in front of the cabin leading the other way."

Carter dropped his hat on his head and ran down the steps, glancing around the yard. "Adam. Adam, come here right now," he called.

The only sound she heard was the rain splattering on the yard and the far-off whinny of the horses.

"Looks like he came here." Carter pointed to the mark of a small boot in the wet ground. "But then, it looks like he went away again, but not back to your cabin."

He kept his eyes on the ground, following the footsteps.

"Did he say anything last night?" Carter asked. "Anything about going anywhere today?"

He sounded so calm. So in charge.

But Emma saw the anxiety in the lines bracketing his mouth.

"No. He just said he wanted to finish the fort today because..." Her voice faltered there. One thing at a time. Find Adam. Deal with Carter later.

Carter chewed at his lip, his eyes skittering around the yard, his hands resting on his hips, his frown deepening. "Yesterday he talked about going up to that old abandoned prospector cabin and getting some stuff out of there." He walked away from Emma, his eyes on the ground.

All Emma wanted to do was run to the corral and grab a horse, jump on it and ride off. Call 911. Do something. Anything. Find her son.

But she had no plan, and she sensed Carter did.

"Here. His prints again." Carter knelt down and pointed to another set of footprints leading away from the yard. "Looks like he's heading up to the hills." Carter turned back to the yard. "Let's saddle up the horses. You take Diamond and I'll take Elijah. He's faster than Banjo."

Finally. A job to do.

She squelched her other fears. Because to go up to the hills, Adam had to cross the river.

Emma headed to the tack shed, slipping in the mud. It seemed to take hours to saddle up the horses with fingers clumsy with fear and cold. Then, finally they were up and riding away from the ranch.

They came to the river, and fear clutched Emma with an icy hand. *Please, Lord, don't let him have fallen into the river. Please, Lord, keep him safe. Please, Lord, let us find him. Please.*

Carter stopped by the river and rode away from the bridge downstream. Then he passed Emma and rode upstream.

Then without a word to Emma, he led his horse across the footbridge, Elijah's shod hooves beating out a muffled rhythm on the wooden bridge. Emma followed.

"Are you sure that's where he would be going?" Emma called out as they rode up the hill. What if Adam had left the yard going down the road? What if they were heading away from him?

Carter didn't answer, his head down, water dripping off his hat onto his broad shoulders. Then a few feet after they got off the bridge, he pointed down. As Emma rode by, she saw it too. The remains of a print in the dirt.

Her son's boot.

Carter flexed his fingers inside his sodden gloves, unclenched his teeth, lowered his shoulders. At least Adam had made it safely across the river. As far as he could guess, the boy had gone to the cabin. They would find him there, give him trouble for making them so scared. They would have a reunion, and then he could talk to Emma about his plans.

Carter stifled his panic as he shifted in his saddle, looking back.

Emma hunched over the saddle, looking down at the trail, water dripping off her hat. As if sensing his gaze on her, she looked up, but her cheeks were pale and her eyes shone with a frantic light.

He wanted to reassure her that everything would be all right. But his own worries were like a howling storm that he struggled to stay on top of.

Please, Lord. Please, Lord.

His prayers were no more than this two-word plea as he pushed Elijah on up the trail that grew more muddy with each passing minute. It couldn't happen again. He couldn't lose another—

There. Another track. Fainter now.

Please, Lord.

He needed to keep his wits about him and keep himself calm and in control. He had to reassure himself that Adam was okay. He couldn't panic. Emma depended on him.

Old doubts and fears spiraled up and with them even more desperate prayers.

You're not the right person for the job. You were gone when Harry died. You couldn't keep Sylvia safe.

This is different. You're doing something about this. You're going to look for him.

The rain battered at them when they were in the open and dripped relentlessly off the trees when they were sheltered. Carter's shirt underneath his slicker grew damp, and his pants were now completely soaked. He should have taken the time to get his leather chaps.

There hadn't been time. There had only been fear and the thought that time was running out.

He nudged Elijah in the ribs, and his horse pushed forward again, head down, feet churning in the mud of the trail.

After what felt like hours, the trail turned out into the open area where the cows were pastured. Carter's mind flicked back to that perfect afternoon as they watched the calves racing across the pasture. As he held Emma in his arms and kissed her.

The day his life had made a drastic shift.

Now he was riding up in these same hills looking for her son, struggling to keep his own worries for the boy at bay.

He pushed on.

Finally he saw the break in the trees, and a few moments later Carter pulled up to the cabin, slid off his horse and tied him up with a few quick twists of the halter rope.

He arrived at the door almost the same time as Emma.

"Adam," she called out as Carter yanked open the door.

The interior of the cabin was gloomy and dank, and Carter had to strain his eyes to see.

A collapsed wooden bed sat in one corner of the cabin, a table pushed up against the wall. A few muddy footprints were on the floor, and water dripped into the cabin from the various holes in the roof.

Carter couldn't see Adam.

"Adam. Adam." Emma's voice, hoarse with fear, echoed in the empty building.

She turned to Carter, catching him by the arms. "Where is he? Where is Adam?"

Carter wanted to pull her into his arms. To hold her close and protect her, but right now they had other concerns.

His gaze swept over the cabin. Think. Think.

Then he noticed that the lanterns that Adam had wanted so badly for the tree fort were gone.

"He's been here." Carter struggled to absorb the information. To sift through it and figure out where Adam could be.

"But where is he now? We didn't see him on the trail. What if he wandered off the trail and we passed him?"

Carter laid his finger on her lips, stopping the spill of panic. "He would have heard us, or the horses would have seen him. He wouldn't have gone off the trail. He didn't on the way up here, he wouldn't have on the way back."

Her face was wet, and he suspected not all the moisture on her cheeks were rain.

"We'll find him, Emma. I promise you."

Please, Lord. Please, Lord.

Emma choked back a sob and dashed her hand over her face. Then she pulled in a quavering breath and glanced around the cabin.

"So where would he have gone?"

Carter had to still his own rising fear as he tried to think. He glanced around the cabin again then stepped outside.

Please, Lord. Please, Lord. Let us find him.

He concentrated on the ground, looking for a clue. Under the trees around the cabin the ground wasn't as wet.

Then he saw it. Another footprint. This one didn't head down the trail back to the ranch. It went up.

"Did you ever tell Adam about the abandoned mine up in the hills?" he asked Emma.

"Wade did when we first came up here. I think he pointed it out to him."

Bingo.

"I think I know where Adam is."

Emma clung to the confidence in Carter's voice even harder than she clung to the saddle horn as they worked their way up the narrow mountain trail. The horses slipped and slid but kept on going.

Rain dripped from her hat brim down the back of her neck, and her pants were so wet and chilled she couldn't feel her thighs.

None of it mattered. All she wanted was to see Adam, to know that he was safe. Their little battle of last night seemed so small and petty now. Why didn't she go up with him to the cabin last night? It would have taken an hour with the horses.

Because he was exhausted and needed his sleep.

So why didn't you go get the lantern?

Because I couldn't leave him alone.

Her mental conversations flipped back and forth between rational reasoning and unreasoning fear.

Please, Lord, let him be okay. Please don't take him from me too.

Her prayer held a note of desperation, and as she prayed she lifted her head, her eyes glued to Carter's back. He looked straight ahead, urging his horse on, as if he couldn't get to the site fast enough.

"There it is," Carter called out, raising his voice above the rain falling on the trees. He pointed as he looked back, and Emma saw it too. The cave opening.

Carter was already out of the saddle, tying up his horse before Emma, cold and stiff and wet, could even lift her leg out of the stirrup. She dismounted, dropped the reins, then charged up the incline behind Carter.

He was in the cave before she scrambled to the opening.

"He's here, Emma. He's here." Carter's voice sounded shaky. "He's all right."

It was only adrenaline that got Emma to the cave, because the relief flooding through her loosened her bones. She staggered into the cave behind Carter, looking wildly around in the half-light. Then she saw a bundle curled up against the wall.

"Adam. Oh, Adam." She stumbled toward him, but Carter was there already, checking him over.

"He's okay," Carter said, sitting back on his haunches, his hands falling to his sides as if they were too heavy to hold up.

Emma crouched down beside her son, then lifted him into her arms. He groaned. Then his eyes opened and he smiled.

"Mommy. I got the lantern."

"Did you? That's great." She pulled him tightly against her, rocking him, tears of relief and gratitude spilling from her eyes.

"Thank You, Lord," she whispered, stroking Adam's head, kissing his cool cheeks. "Thank You."

Adam pulled back. "Why are you crying, Mommy?"

Emma sniffed and swiped her gloved hand over her eyes. "Because I thought you were lost," she said, her fear slowly melting away now that she knew he was safe. "I woke up this morning and you weren't in your bed. I thought something bad had happened."

Adam lowered his head. "I just wanted to get the lantern, and you said you wouldn't. So I thought I would get it before you woked up."

"Oh, honey," Emma said, her voice wobbly with relief.

"You should have told us," Carter said. "That was very dangerous for you to come up here all by yourself."

Emma caught the strained tone of Carter's voice. As if this was too close to his own loss.

"I'm sorry," Adam mumbled. "I won't do it again."

"Why did you come up here?" Carter asked.

"It was raining and the cabin was wet. I remembered Wade told me about the cave."

"It's okay, honey. We found you," she said, her own voice trembling with relief. "I'm so glad you stayed here," she said. "That you didn't go wandering off." She drew gently back and stroked his hair away from his face. "I was so worried about you."

"I'm sorry, Mommy." He bit his lip, and Emma could see that he was close to tears himself. She forced herself to stand and pulled him up with her.

"I know you are, but you know what? Now we have to go back to the ranch."

Adam spun his head around, looking. "My lantern. Where's my lantern? We have to go get it."

"We need to go right back to the ranch," Carter said,

the firm note in his voice brooking no argument. "We can come back for that another time."

"But I came up here to get the lantern."

"Adam—"

Carter and Emma spoke at the same time. Carter held up his hand. "Sorry. I didn't mean to—"

"It's okay." Emma gave him a smile of understanding. She didn't mind his interjection. In spite of the tension they had just experienced, his behavior with Adam created another connection with Carter. It was as if, for the first time in her life, she had help and support in taking care of her son.

Emma zipped up Adam's jacket, hoping it would be warm enough. "Okay. Let's go," she said, tugging his hat down on his head.

They stepped out into the rain which, if anything, had increased in the past few minutes. Thankfully the trip down would take less time than it took coming up—and with a lot less stress.

"Adam should probably ride with you on the trip home," Carter suggested. "I don't trust Elijah with two people."

Emma nodded and climbed into the saddle. She sat back as far as she could then held out her arms for Adam. Carter set him in front of Emma. Diamond jigged a bit but settled as Emma tugged lightly on the reins. Carter smiled up at her, and she read a promise in his eyes. When they came back to the ranch, they would talk.

Once Carter was in the saddle, Emma turned and led the way down the mountain back to the ranch. They were going home. The thought made her smile.

The trail had gotten muddier since they had gone up, and Diamond slid a few times. But Emma trusted him to keep his footing and for the most part let him have his head.

But all the while they rode she felt Carter behind them, protecting them, watching out for them.

After what felt like an eternity, the trail made one more turn and then, through a break in the trees, she saw the ranch.

"See, honey. We're almost home," she said to Adam, shivering with relief and the cold. "We just have to cross the river and we're home."

They got to the creek, and Emma's heart dropped like a stone.

The bridge was washed out and the river, once a benign babbling stream of water had swollen to almost twice its size and had become a raging swirl of logs and muddied water.

Carter pulled up beside her, and Emma read the concern on his face. He glanced upstream then down. "This is the best place to cross," he said, raising his voice above the noise of the creek and the rain. "Farther up it's too narrow, and farther down it gets too rocky and steep."

"I'll go first," Emma called out, pushing down her own trepidation. "Diamond is sure-footed."

Carter still didn't look convinced, but they both knew there was no other option. He put his hand on her arm, his own fingers blue with cold. "You be careful. I'll be praying for you."

Emma gave him a tight smile, sent up her own prayer for safety, then nudged Diamond in the side and loosened the reins to give him more freedom.

Diamond shook his head then, when Emma nudged him again, took a tentative step into the water. Emma tried not to look at the water gushing past them, her heart fluttering in her chest, her breath coming in quick gasps.

She felt the force of the swelling water against Diamond's body as he took one cautious step after another.

Just a few more feet, she thought, trying not to urge him on. Just a bit more.

"Emma. Watch out," Carter shouted, his voice urgent.

She turned in time to see the log surging toward them. Before she could react, it hit Diamond. He lost his footing, and Emma and Adam were plunged into the icy water.

Chapter Thirteen

There was no time to think. No time to plan.

Carter threw off his slicker and plunged into the river. The cold sucked the air out of him, and it was all he could do to keep his head above the water.

A wave washed over him and he came up, sputtering, his eyes filmed with dirty water.

Where were they? Where did they go?

There. Downstream. Too far.

He saw Emma's head bobbing, her arm flailing. Where was Adam?

Please, Lord. Please not again.

He dug his arms in the water, pulling, swimming and then, miraculously, he was closer. With one final lunge, he caught Emma by the jacket.

He couldn't talk. Couldn't say anything above the roar of the water. He kicked and swam, trying to find purchase on the slippery rocks.

They inched closer to the bank with each stroke of his arm, each kick of his feet. Was it soon enough?

The river made a tight turn farther downstream, then plunged down a series of rocky rapids. They had to get to shore before the turn.

One more pull. One more kick. Emma swam too.

He caught an overhanging branch with his free arm, but the force of the river almost tore the branch out of his hand.

He held on, praying, sputtering as water washed over them. And inch by inch, he hauled his precious burden closer to shore.

Emma finally managed to get her feet under her. She was up to her thighs in the water and the flowing stream pulled at her slicker, but she was safe. Carter looked back out to the water.

He couldn't see Adam.

Carter's fear became a black, whirling vortex.

Emma was pulled sideways, but she managed to grab a branch from the tree Carter had caught, and she rose up out of the water again.

And Carter saw she was holding Adam by his jacket.

"Is he okay?" Carter gasped as they moved forward foot by foot, working their way up the tree's branches.

Emma only nodded, water streaming down her face, her eyes two dark brown bruises in her chalk-white face as they worked their way to shore.

Then, finally, the water's force lessened. They were up to their knees, then their ankles and then Carter could help Emma lift Adam up and onto the soggy grass of the bank.

He lay quiet, then he sat up, coughed and sputtered, and Carter's bones went rubbery with relief.

"Carter? Mom?" Adam called out, looking wildly around, water streaming down his face. He blinked and rubbed his eyes, and then Emma crouched down beside him, her hair plastered to her face, her lips blue with the cold.

Carter had never seen a more beautiful sight in his life.

"We're here," Emma said then coughed herself. "We're all here."

Carter caught Adam and held him close, rocking him, and then tears, warm against his ice-cold cheeks, poured down his face. "I'm so glad you're okay, little guy. So glad."

Emma knelt beside him and he grabbed her with his free arm, pulling them all together in a circle of life. They embraced and laughed and cried. There were not enough emotions to express what they had just gone through.

Then Emma caught Carter's face in her hands and pressed a cold, wet kiss on his mouth. "Thank you. Thank you," she sobbed, her voice hoarse, her eyes red with tears and river water.

Carter kissed her back. He couldn't hold her close enough. Couldn't kiss her enough. They were all here. They were all alive. *Thank You, Lord,* he prayed. *Thank You.*

He could say nothing more.

"I was really scared," Adam said as Emma toweled him off, steam from the warm bath still hovering in the room. "I thought I was going to be drownded."

Emma shut her mind off to the images flooding her mind because of his innocent comment. She had to pin her attention to the here. The now. Concentrate on rubbing the moisture out of her precious son's hair, wrapping the towel around his warm, pink body.

His wriggling, living body. He was okay. Everything was okay. Carter had saved them.

"You're nice and clean now," she said with a forced smile. "That mud from our walk all washed off you."

After they came out of the river, the three of them had

walked for a few hundred yards, shivering and holding each other up, the horses following docilely behind them.

Emma still couldn't believe that Diamond had managed to scramble to shore or that Elijah had forded the river on his own. All that was another reason for thanks.

By the time they arrived at the ranch, they weren't shivering as hard, but the chill had settled deep in Emma's bones.

Carter had tried to make Emma take a shower at his grandmother's place while he took care of Adam, but she didn't want to let Adam out of her sight.

"There, now you look as shiny as a new penny," she said, bending over to plant a kiss on his forehead.

"When can we get my lantern?" Adam asked.

After everything that happened, all he could talk about was a lantern?

He's only five, she reminded herself. *He moves past and moves on.*

"We're not getting it for a long time," Emma replied, fear making her voice more authoritative than usual.

Now that everyone was okay and they were safe and warm, she felt the need to lay down the law.

"You shouldn't have taken off like that." She kept her voice quiet but firm.

Adam dropped his head. "I said I was sorry."

Emma knelt down and tilted his face up to hers. "I know you are, honey. But I was so scared when I woke up and didn't see you there. You know that you never, ever go out of the cabin without me."

Adam kept his eyes averted, and though Emma could see he was sorry, she felt she had to drive this point home.

It could have ended so badly. It could have been so much worse. An icy shiver trickled down her spine at the memory of what they had just survived.

"This is important, Adam. You know what I'm saying, don't you?"

Adam gave a tiny nod, and Emma saw tears welling up in his eyes. She steeled herself to his sorrow.

"Because you went out without me and didn't tell anyone, we are not going to be working on the tree fort for the rest of the week."

Adam blinked and a tear, released from his eye, trickled down his cheek. He sniffed and wiped his face with the back of his hand.

"Carter isn't going to be here anyway," he said quietly.

Emma didn't want to think about what Adam was saying. Carter had given her no indication he was leaving.

Like you had much time for chitchat.

But surely he would have said something. Even on the way back to the ranch?

Yeah, something like, it's been fun saving your life and all, but I got to do what I got to do?

"Then *I'm* not going to be helping you with your tree fort," Emma corrected, trying to still the panic that hovered. Carter wasn't leaving. She was sure of that.

She pushed herself to her feet and brought him out to the living room, determined to carry on. "You're allowed to watch *Backyardigans* while I have a quick shower."

She stopped and tightened her grip on his shoulder, which made Adam look up at her in concern.

"You're not leaving the house, are you?"

"I won't do it again, Mommy," he said, suddenly subdued. "I don't want to be scared like that again."

A picture flashed through her mind. Adam falling off the horse, her swimming after him. The panic that paralyzed her even after she caught his coat.

Then Carter's hand grabbed her, and their relentless surging down the river stopped. She closed her eyes, preferring to focus on that moment when she and Carter held Adam and each other on the riverbank. After he had saved their lives.

She went back to the bathroom and made quick work of her own shower. The hot water washing over her removed the memory of the cold and the fear. She deliberately pushed back the doubts that Adam's words had planted in her mind. Until she heard from Carter herself, she wasn't going to speculate on what was happening after this.

Adam still sat on the couch when she came back, toweling off her hair. He was watching the show, smiling faintly at the antics of the cartoon characters.

She sat quietly beside him, brushing her hair, her own mind wandering to Carter in Nana Beck's house. Should she go to him? Wait for him to come here?

Ten minutes passed. Twenty. Thirty.

Surely he was done now. Surely Nana Beck would realize he would want to come here to make sure they were okay.

Emma closed her eyes, reliving that moment when he kissed her. When she kissed him back.

I want to talk to you.

His voice resonated through her head, adding to her growing concern. He wouldn't leave now, would he? Not when the assurance of a future hung between them, unspoken but present.

Finally she couldn't stand it any longer. "Put on your coat, mister," she said to her son. "We're going to find Carter."

When they stepped out of the house, the rain had quit, but rivulets of water flowed into the flower garden.

They ran across the yard, splashing through the puddles. Each step held apprehension and created an inevitable movement toward something she might not want to face.

They knocked on Nana's door and, without waiting for a reply, stepped inside.

The homey scent of coffee and cookies baking comforted her, creating a sense of normalcy. A solid reassurance in a frightening and emotional morning.

"Hello," Emma called out in her brightest, happiest voice. As she shucked off her coat, she glanced quickly around the entrance.

She didn't see Carter's boots or his coat, and as they walked into the kitchen, she didn't see him.

Nana Beck was already coming toward them, her arms spread wide, her eyes registering her concern.

"Oh, my dear children," she said, hugging first Emma then Adam, the comforting scent of vanilla and chocolate wafting around them. "Carter told me what happened. You must have been so frightened. I'm so thankful you're okay." She pressed her hand to her heart, and Emma was afraid that she might have another attack.

"We're fine. It's okay," she assured her, grasping her by the shoulder. "Really."

Nana's eyes glistened. "I'm so thankful. So thankful." She drew in an unsteady breath, then forced a smile to her face. "Do you want some hot chocolate and cookies?"

What Emma really wanted was Carter, but she wasn't telling Nana Beck that. Emma glanced around the kitchen again as maybe, by some weird chance, Carter was hiding in a room somewhere.

Nana set a kettle of water on the stove and then put out two mugs. One for her and one for Adam.

Emma couldn't stand the tension one second longer.

"Where's Carter? He told me he was going to wash up here."

Nana nodded. "He did. And then he left."

"He left? For his cabin?" Emma couldn't keep the sharp note out of her voice.

"He said he had to go to town. I thought he told you?"

"No. He didn't tell me a thing."

"Well, now. That's a puzzle." Nana Beck's words and her accompanying frown sent Emma's heart plunging into her stomach. Why didn't he stop to talk to her? Why did he leave right away?

She and Adam stayed long enough to eat cookies and drink the chocolate. As soon as was polite, Emma retreated to her cabin and her worries.

Chapter Fourteen

"I don't want to bake bread. I want to go to work on my tree fort." Adam dropped into a chair by the kitchen table of Wade and Miranda's house and heaved out a sigh.

"I know you do, but it's going to be dark in a while, and I have to get this bread done," Emma said, trying to keep her voice soothing as she sent yet another glance out the window at the setting sun.

Carter was gone on his bike again.

Unbidden came the feeling of his arms around her after he had pulled her and Adam out of the river. Too easily, she again felt the blinding fear and choking panic.

Carter had saved them. And then Carter had left. He'd been gone all afternoon. It was seven o'clock now, and he still hadn't returned.

Don't trust men, don't trust men.

Emma felt a cold place in the center of her chest that had once harbored affection. Attraction. Maybe even love. Now, all that lived there was the pain of being left behind. Again.

She had trusted Carter. She had opened up to him and let him into her life. Now he was gone without a word.

She poured water into the bowl Miranda always used

for bread, measured out the yeast and put in the sugar, just like Miranda had taught her.

She wasn't even sure why she was doing this. But she had to keep herself busy, as she had all afternoon. After they left Nana Beck's, she and Adam had cleaned out their cabin. Then they came to the house and tidied it up.

Busy work, Emma thought, taking the eggs out of the refrigerator.

"I'm bored," Adam whined, swinging his feet. "I don't know what to do."

"You can help me make bread," she said with a falsely bright smile.

"That's boring." He draped himself over the table, dropping his chin on his arms. "When is Carter coming back?"

Emma bit back a snappy response to that as she measured out the oil. She wanted Carter to come back too. So she could give him a piece of her mind.

And then, so she could quit. She needed to get on with her own life, and when he came back—whenever that would be—she and Adam were going to leave. She couldn't be with a man who ran whenever things got difficult.

But he pulled you from the river. He saved your life.

And what else could he have done? Why didn't he stay to see how she and Adam were doing? To talk about what happened to them? To help her deal with it?

In spite of her questions and her frustration with Carter, the thought of leaving him sent a shaft of pain into her heart. Into her very soul.

Carter. His face swam into her mind, and right behind that came a wave of sorrow mixed with anger.

How could he just walk away after all that had happened? Was he too scared to face them? Had he shown them too much of himself? Was he pulling back emotionally, as well as physically?

Her eyes closed as her heart and mind battled with each other. Karl's betrayal had hurt, but she had gotten through it.

She knew, deep in her soul, that Carter's absence after what they had just shared hurt far more.

Please, Lord, help me to find my peace in You. Help me to trust in You only. Only You are faithful.

She waited a moment, reaching for the peace that she had prayed for. Drawing in a long, slow breath, she straightened.

Keep going. Do what comes next. Get through this. Keep busy.

Then, as she took the flour out of the pantry, she heard a noise that lifted her heart. Was that a bike?

She shook her head, angry at how easily her hope was resurrected.

The noise grew and became the distinctive sound of a motorbike. Her heart jumped as she dropped the bag of flour on the counter, then leaned over the sink to look out the window.

There he was, parking his bike and pulling off his helmet.

Just like he had the first time she saw him. Only, then she didn't know who he was. Now, the sight of that thick, wavy hair catching the light from the setting sun, that shadowed jaw and his slate-blue eyes brought a flush to her cheeks and sent anticipation singing through her veins.

She pulled back from the window, clenching her fists, trying to pull her emotions to a more neutral place.

The door opened, and Adam's head shot up.

"Carter! You're back!" Adam shot out of the chair and

threw himself at the tall figure that entered the house, his presence taking over the kitchen.

Carter bent over and caught Adam under his arms, swung him up in the air then, to Emma's surprise, pulled him close in a fierce hug.

Then, dropping Adam onto his hip, he turned to Emma.

"Hey, there," he said, his voice quiet. "How are you? Feeling okay?"

Her eyes blurred and her throat thickened, and she turned away so he couldn't see how his presence and the concern in his voice affected her.

"I'm fine. So is Adam." She cracked open the eggs with unnecessary force, almost sending the contents of the bowl spewing over the counter.

"That was really scary when we were in the water," Adam said, wrapping his arms around Carter's neck. "I'm so glad you saved us."

Emma glanced over in time to see Carter hold Adam close, his eyes closed, his arms wrapped tightly around the little body. The sight of him holding her son created a tiny bloom of warmth, thawing the chill that she had wrapped herself in for protection. "I'm glad too, buddy," Carter said.

Adam put up with the hug for a minute, but then pulled away, his eyes holding Carter's. "Were you scared?"

Emma caught fear in Carter's broken gaze. Then he nodded. "Yes. I was scared."

"But you were really brave," Adam said.

"So were you," Carter replied, then let his eyes rest on Emma. "And so was your mother."

"Where did you go after you brought us back? My mommy was mad at you for going away."

Emma tore her gaze away from Carter, but didn't bother to reprimand her son. He was only telling the truth.

"Adam, can you go tell Nana Beck that I'm here?" Carter said quietly, setting Adam on the floor. "Ask her to give you some of her cookies and wait for me there."

Adam glanced from Emma to Carter, unsure whether to follow the instructions. Not that Emma blamed him. Hadn't she spent all day reminding him that he wasn't to go anywhere without her?

"I'll go with you. To make sure you get there okay," Carter said. "It's getting dark out there."

So Carter and Adam left, and for a few moments Emma was alone to try to gather her thoughts and scattered emotions.

She pressed her hands to her heated cheeks, angry at the tears that threatened, a sign of how much Carter had come to mean to her in the past few weeks.

Keep it together, she scolded herself. *Don't cave.*

A few minutes later, Carter was back. He stood in the doorway of the kitchen of his old house, and, in spite of her confusion in his presence, she felt a flicker of sympathy for him. How hard it must be to see a woman and a child, the same age as his son, in his house.

Would Harry and Sylvia's memories always hang over this place? Could he ever forget them and simply see her and Adam?

"Can I come in?" Carter asked, his voice quiet.

Emma nodded and beat the eggs into the oil. But Carter didn't go to the table and sit on the chair. He came to stand beside her, resting his hip against the counter, looking down on her.

"I'm sorry," was all he said. "I'm sorry I had to leave."

Emma swallowed a knot of sorrow, wishing his pres-

ence didn't affect her so. Then, unable to keep her eyes
down, she looked over at him.

"Why did you have to leave? And why did you stay
away?" The questions burst out of her, edged with frustration and sorrow.

Carter waited a moment, as if gathering his thoughts
in the face of her emotions. "I had to go to the real-estate
agent," he said. "And I had to get there as soon as possible. I'm sorry I wasn't here for you, but I had to do something very important."

She turned her attention back to the flour she was measuring out. "What was so important?"

Carter released a heavy sigh. "When I put the ranch up
for sale, Pete gave me an escape clause. I had until noon
today to call if I wanted to cancel the sale. But I missed
that call."

Emma's hands slowed as she tried to absorb what he
was telling her.

"What do you mean you missed the call?"

Carter took the measuring cup out of her hands and set
it on the countertop. He took her hands in his and pressed
them. "When you came to my cabin this morning, I was
leaving for town, remember?"

Emma's mind ticked back, recalling Carter's pressed
shirt, his new jeans. He had been dressed to go out. "But
that was when Adam was missing." Things fell into place.
"And we went out to get him." She stopped there, the
memory of what had happened too fresh and frighten-
ingly real.

"When we got back to the ranch, I was already late.
I wanted to talk to Pete about canceling the sale, but by
then, it was past noon. I went into town, hoping that I
could talk to him face-to-face, work something out.
Change things."

Emma's confusion settled and reality took its place. "You wanted to cancel the sale of the ranch? Why?"

Carter reached up and fingered a strand of hair away from her face, his fingers trailing down her cheek, then coming to rest on her shoulder. "I didn't want to let it go. I wanted it to be mine. For you and Adam and me."

She held his gaze, unable to speak, as his words settled like oil on the troubled waters of her soul.

"When I found out I couldn't stop the sale," he continued, "I tried to come up with another plan. To fix what I had broken." His eyes traveled over her face, regret etched on his features. "I wanted to make a home for us."

Weakness invaded Emma's limbs as hope unfurled in her chest. "A home? Here?"

Carter nodded, his hands moving to her waist, holding her up.

Emma bit her lip, his touch confusing and comforting her at the same time. "I thought…when you left…that you weren't coming back."

Desolation crept over Carter's features. "Did you think I would leave you like Adam's father left you?"

His words lay bare her deepest fears. "I trusted him to take care of us," she said, looking down at her hands. "Trusted him to do the right thing. Then, one day, he just left. And Adam and I were alone."

His hands tightened their grip on her waist. "I'm so sorry. I should have called you, but when we got to the ranch and I realized the time, I was in such a hurry to get to town that I left my phone behind. Then, when I found out I couldn't stop the sale, I was too upset to call. I never even thought that you would assume I was leaving for good." He tipped her chin up with a finger. "I was coming back. I figured you would know that."

Emma couldn't hold his gaze, her own shame intruding

on the moment. "Every man in my life, other than Adam, has let me down. I was afraid you had done the same."

"Even after I rescued you?"

She was surprised to hear the faint note of humor in his voice, but as her gaze slid to his, she caught a hint of fear in his eyes, a hint of the fear she had heard in his voice when he pulled them out of the river.

"Even after you rescued me," she echoed.

Silence followed her comment, then Carter spoke. "I know I wasn't the best person when you first met me, but I've changed. And you're the one who helped me make that change. I've come to care for you and Adam more than I ever thought I could. I didn't want to fall for you. Didn't want to let you into my life, but you found a way in." He slipped his hands to the small of her back, closing the small distance between them. "When you and Adam fell into the river, I thought I'd lost you both. I thought that was it." His voice stumbled over the words, as if re-living the pain the moment had caused. "Then, when I jumped in and saved you, I knew it wasn't over. I hadn't lost someone else I cared so deeply for."

Was it true? Did he care deeply for her?

Then she looked up at him, and in his eyes, she saw a yearning that sent her heart hammering.

But he had more to say.

"You scared me, Emma. You and Adam. But when we came to the other side, I knew, more than anything, that I had to find a way to keep us together. To keep us on the ranch that I know you love, and that I've always loved— just not always appreciated. That's why I left. I left for you. For us."

His words, spoken with such authority, eased into her lost and lonely soul.

"I want you to trust me, Emma. To trust that I will take care of you. I can only hope that you believe me."

Emma felt a prickling behind her eyes as she clung to his words. She drew in an unsteady breath, struggling to find her way through this new, unfamiliar place. "I'm sorry I thought you left me. I…I haven't had a lot of reasons to trust men. Adam's father left as soon as he found out I was pregnant. My father let me down by gambling away our ranch, leaving Adam and me with nothing. My old boyfriend cheated on me. When I came here, I didn't trust men, and didn't want to." Her sudden resolve faltered as old fears and distrusts intruded.

Carter said nothing for a moment, as if honoring her confession. "I'm sorry you thought that of me," he said quietly. "I don't know what to say to make you believe you can trust me." He stopped there and his hand came up and traced the line of her cheek. His touch was tentative, as if unsure of her reaction.

Emma looked up at him as other pictures imposed themselves. Carter in church. Carter holding Adam as if he was his own. Carter trusting her enough with his sorrow to cry in her arms, letting her see his broken places.

Carter risking his own life to save her and her son.

Emma felt her body relax, as if she'd been struggling to carry a weight and could finally release her burden. She looked back up at Carter and felt as if she was balanced on a precipice, that things could shift either way depending on what she said or did next.

In a moment of blinding clarity, she knew which way she wanted to go. Maybe it was too soon, but she knew if she didn't tell him now, she never would.

"I trust you, Carter Beck," she said, sincerity ringing

in her voice, "with me and my son. I trust you with our lives, and I trust you with our hearts."

The silence following her declaration grew large, heavy, and for a moment Emma wondered if she had said too much. Exposed her heart too fully.

Then he swept her in his arms, cradled her head in his hand and kissed her. Hard. Then again. Then more gently, as if sealing a promise.

He drew her close, laying her head against his chest, his chin resting on her head. His chest lifted in a sigh, and Emma closed her eyes, contentment washing over her.

She wanted time to stop right here. Right now. She didn't want to think what may lay ahead or what they would have to deal with once the ranch sold.

Carter rubbed his chin over her head. "Thank you," he whispered. "Thank you for trusting me."

She drew back and, smiling up at him, brushed a lock of hair back from his forehead, as if sealing a claim on him. "I didn't think I could put my trust in a man again. But, yes, I trust you."

He kissed her again, then rested his hands on her shoulders, his expression growing serious. "And I love you."

Emma stared as the words, one by one, dropped into her weary soul.

"Did…did I hear you right?"

Carter stroked her hair back from her face, his fingers lingering on her cheek as his mouth lifted in a wistful smile. "Yeah. You did." He released a short laugh that held a note of melancholy but absolutely no bitterness. "I didn't think I'd ever say those words again. But you kind of snuck up on me.

She didn't want to cry, but she felt her throat thicken

and her eyes grow warm. She blinked, trying to find her footing in this new place.

Carter caught his lower lip between his teeth. "Um… now would be a good time to say something."

"I love you too." She couldn't stop the words and didn't want to. "You opened up my heart and soul again, and I trust you with both," she said quietly.

Carter pressed another kiss to her lips then drew her close against him. He laid his hand on her head, stroking her hair with his thumb. "I dared to make plans again. Dared to hope we could make a life on this ranch. I'm so sorry I couldn't stop the sale."

Regret flickered, but only for a moment. Emma wrapped her arms around his waist, holding him close.

"I'm sorry too, but you know, right now I'm thankful for what we have. Right here. You and me and Adam. I'm thankful for all the blessings God has given us. Anything else is only gravy. Extra." She pulled back to gauge his reaction to what she had just said.

Carter's mouth lifted in a wry smile, but Emma saw he wasn't convinced.

"I mean it, Carter," she insisted. "I know it sounds corny, but we have each other, and that's the best starting point."

"I'll have the money from the sale of the ranch. We could start somewhere else…" He shook his head slowly. "I can't believe it's happening. I wish…I wish I hadn't…"

Emma said nothing but pressed her fingers against his lips. "It doesn't matter, Carter. Like I said, we have each other, and that's more than we had even a few weeks ago when you still owned the ranch."

He cupped her shoulders in his hands. "I feel like my life has spun in a completely different direction since then."

"So has mine. But I'm comforted that we're facing that direction together." Regret was still etched on his face. What could she say to assure him? She covered his hands with hers, her gaze seeking his and holding it. "The ranch is just a place. A home and a business."

"You already lost one home and business," Carter said, his voice urgent. "When you had to sell your father's ranch. Now I'm bringing that same disappointment back into your life. I know how much you loved this place, and now I took that away from you too."

"You gave me so much more," she said quietly. "Anyone can build a house. A business. A ranch. But what we have now, what you've just given me, is the most important foundation for any life together. When your great-great-grandfather made his choice, he didn't choose for money. He chose for love. When you chose to help me go find Adam, you made the right choice too. Because if you hadn't…" Her voice faltered as the frightening images flickered through her mind again.

He drew her close, as if to shelter her from the memories.

"I'm so thankful to the Lord for saving us," she continued, speaking from the shelter of his arms. "For using you to save us."

They were quiet a moment, as if letting the moment settle into their minds and their lives.

Emma didn't want to move on. She wished it would never end.

Then the door of the kitchen slammed open and Adam burst into the room. He skidded to a halt when he saw Carter and Emma. He looked from one to the other, and as he did Emma felt her heart falter.

Then he grinned and ran toward them, his arms open wide. "Hug me too, hug me too," he called out, and Carter and Emma bent over and swept him into their arms, completing the circle.

"Well, I'd say that's about time."

Nana Beck's wry voice made them all look up. She stood in the doorway, her arms folded over her midsection, looking smug and well pleased with herself.

Emma endured a moment of guilt. After all, she now stood in the kitchen of the house that had once belonged to Sylvia, her arms around her husband.

But Nana Beck's smile was like a blessing on the moment. A stamp of approval that swept away any misgivings Emma had.

"We were just coming over—"

"Of course you were," Nana Beck said, giving Emma a quick wink. "But Adam was getting impatient and I was getting curious. So now we're here." Nana moved into the kitchen and sat on a nearby chair. "And you might want to do something about that bread dough," she said, angling her head toward the bowl now overflowing with risen dough.

She laughed and reluctantly released herself from Carter's arms. Adam, however, stayed there gladly, asking Carter about the fort and when they were going to work on it again.

Emma stifled her own regret as she and Carter exchanged melancholy glances. But she gave him an encouraging smile before she turned her attention back to her bread. What was done was done. As she had told Carter, they had each other, and that was truly what mattered, wasn't it?

She put a kettle of water on the stove to make some tea. As she returned to her bread, the phone rang.

Carter caught it on the third ring, and as Emma punched down the dough, she couldn't help listening.

Carter's replies were terse, and she didn't get much out of what he said.

Then he hung up the phone, staring at it for a moment. He drew in a long, slow breath, then turned to Emma.

"That was Pete. The buyer is coming tomorrow to look over the ranch."

Chapter Fifteen

"Why have you not laid a water line to the corrals? For your horses." Jurgen Mallik, the buyer of the ranch, tugged on his glaringly white cowboy hat as he stood in the corral, looking around.

Jurgen was spare of build with graying blond hair hanging well below the brim of his cowboy hat. His jeans were new-store crisp, and his blue-and-white plaid shirt still held the fold lines from the packaging Carter suspected it had just come from.

"There is a water line. It's not hooked up to a waterer, though." Carter was surprised how easily the words came out. The underlying pain still lay in his soul, but it was as if it had settled and the edges worn smooth. He caught Emma's look of concern and gave her a quick smile to let her know it was okay. She moved a bit closer to him, as if to make sure.

"You have said you have a manager who has been helping you to take care of this place?" Jurgen asked in his heavily accented English.

"He's out of town on a family emergency now, but he'll be back in a couple of weeks." Carter dropped his hat on his head, hoping he didn't sound as out of breath as he was. Jurgen had come twenty minutes earlier than Pete had told Carter yesterday. Eager to see the place, he had said, apologizing when he had shown up.

Emma, however, chatted with him while they waited. Which was okay with Carter. She knew more about the current ranching operations than he did.

"Wade has been taking care of the ranch while Carter was gone," Pete hastened to explain. "I'm sure he'd be willing to stay on as manager once you take over."

Pete angled a questioning look Carter's way, as if to verify.

"Is this true? Would your man be able to help me with this ranch?" Jurgen asked.

"I can't speak for Wade. You'd have to talk to him about that, but I'm sure he would be pleased to know that he could still work here." Carter was glad Jurgen would be willing to keep Wade on. That had been one of his concerns for his good friend. "You might want to look at hiring an extra hand, though, until you know the ranch well enough to manage it yourself," Carter said.

Jurgen frowned as he looked at Emma. "I understand you work here. You would not be staying on?"

Emma's hand surreptitiously slipped into Carter's. "I don't think so."

Her hesitant words gave Carter pause. After his declaration, they hadn't had much opportunity to talk. To decide where things were going between them. To make any plans. He had his own ideas, but he could hardly expect Emma would immediately fall in with them simply because he had told her he loved her.

Jurgen's eyes slipped to their hands. "I see," he said, though his frown told them otherwise. "So now I have seen the house and the corrals. Now I would like to see the cows."

"They're in the upper pasture," Carter said. "We would have to ride up to them." He glanced over Jurgen's clothes, the cowboy boots so new the soles were probably unscuffed.

"I expect that," Jurgen said. "I have ridden horses before."

Carter doubted that, but he kept his doubts to himself.

"Have you ridden English or Western?" Emma asked.

"English," Jurgen replied. "But the Western saddles are sturdier. I am confident I can hold my seat."

"I can let him ride Diamond," Emma said, as if sensing Carter's hesitation. "We can use Wade's saddle."

This seemed to be the best plan.

"Did you want to come up with us?" Carter asked Pete as Emma got the halters from the tack shed.

He held up his hands, a look of horror on his face. "You kidding me? I'll go see if I can scam some cookies from your grandmother. How long will you be?"

"Maybe half an hour. Probably more."

"Take your time." Pete shot them a quick smile, then beat a hasty retreat.

"So this Emma girl. She is your girlfriend?" Jurgen asked as Carter pulled two saddles off the trees in the tack shed.

Again Carter felt a faint niggle of dissatisfaction. He wanted to lay a claim on Emma, but in spite of what she had said to him yesterday, he still felt as if he had to get part of his own life in order before he did.

And the biggest part was what to do after the ranch was sold. He wanted to know he could provide for her and Adam. Take care of them.

How was he supposed to do that when his future and future employment were surrounded by so much uncertainty?

"We care for each other," was all he said as he laid the saddles by the hitching post.

He looked up to see Emma coming toward them, leading three horses through the grass. The sun burnished her brown hair, bringing out a reddish tinge. She was talking to the horses, her voice low, quiet and confident.

This was where she belonged, Carter thought, his heart growing heavy in his chest. If only…

He cut that thought off. The new owner of the ranch stood in front of him, waiting to be shown the rest of the place. Carter had spent enough time in the past. It was now time to move on.

Twenty minutes later they were mounted up, and Emma led them out of the pasture toward the river.

"Pete tells me the ranch has been in your family for four generations," Jurgen was saying as they rode side by side down the trail.

"That's true. My great-great-grandfather started this place, and it's been passed on." Carter tried to keep his voice even, his tone light, but regret hung like a cloud in the background. Why had he been so hasty? Why hadn't he waited?

"I asked Pete why you are selling this place. He only told me that you had experienced a loss."

"My son. He drowned in a stock waterer in the corral two years ago." Again Carter felt the pain of the words, but as he spoke them he looked ahead and saw Emma sitting straight in the saddle, her hand resting on her thigh. She didn't wear a hat this time, but her pose so easily resurrected his first memory of her.

How much had changed since then. Emma had brought such healing into his life.

As they splashed across the river, much lower now than a few days ago, Emma looked back, giving him a tentative smile, as if quietly thanking him again for saving her and Adam. He returned the smile, and in that moment his regret slipped away.

They would make it, he thought. It didn't matter where he, Emma and Adam lived or what they did. They would make it because they would be together.

"I am so sorry to hear about your son," Jurgen said quietly as the horses walked up the other bank of the river. "That is a huge loss and difficult to recuperate from."

"It was, but I'm thankful for Emma and her son, Adam," Carter replied. "They've given me a new reason to carry on."

Jurgen said nothing after that. The trail narrowed and they rode single file. Once in a while Emma turned around and pointed something out to Jurgen. A mountain they saw through the trees. An old wagon trail, since overgrown. Rubbings on the tree from elk trying to shed the velvet from their antlers.

The sun played hide-and-seek behind the clouds, but as they broke out of the trees into the open fields of the upper pastures, the clouds dissipated. Golden sun poured down from a blue sky and lit up the valley below like a promise.

"Nydelig utsikt," Jurgen said, his voice full of awe as he brought Diamond to a halt. He leaned forward, his eyes looking over the valley as shadows of clouds chased each other over the green-clad slopes of the mountains sweeping away from them. The dumbfounded expression on his face said more than his words had.

"I don't think we need a translation of that," Emma said as she brought Dusty up beside Carter's horse. "I remember feeling exactly the same way when I first saw this."

Carter gave her a melancholy smile then, giving in to

an impulse, brushed her hair back from her face. His fingers lingered a moment on her cheek, and she reached up and captured his hand in hers.

"I'm so sorry. I wish things were different."

She squeezed his hand, her expression growing serious. "No. Please. Don't say that. We've both spent enough time in the past. I don't want you to look back."

He cupped her cheek with his hand, and his smile shifted. "How did I get so blessed to have you come into my life?"

"How many acres—" Jurgen stopped, and Carter dragged his attention away from Emma.

"I'm sorry," Carter said, lowering his hand. "What were you going to ask?"

Jurgen's eyes slid from Carter to Emma, as if trying to puzzle out their relationship.

"I was wondering how many acres you have up here. For pasture. And how many cows the pasture can carry."

Carter shot Emma an inquiring glance. "Why don't you take care of this?" he asked. "You're the one who came up with the rotational-grazing plan."

"Rotational grazing?" Jurgen frowned again.

Emma swung off her saddle. "Come with me," she said. "I'll explain."

Jurgen dismounted and followed Emma, but Carter stayed behind, looking out over the valley. Thankfully it was too early in the day to see The Shadow Woman. He was afraid that if she made an appearance, he would see rebuke in her features.

In spite of Emma's brave words, mourning of another sort settled in his soul. Mourning for the loss of a place where he grew up. A place that had been a source of refuge for him and his brother. A place where he and his cousins had grown up.

Naomi had called him early this morning and had expressed her regret at the loss of the ranch, but she had echoed what Emma had said. The ranch was just a place. People were what counted.

And yet…

Carter tried to slough off his momentary funk.

Forgive me, Lord, he prayed. *Help me to be thankful in all circumstances.*

Then he looked back at Emma, and he realized how blessed he really was.

"…we get better usage of the land and the cows are healthier," she was saying, obviously selling Jurgen on her new project.

Carter came up beside Emma, and she flashed him a quick smile. He caught her hand in his, giving it a gentle squeeze.

"What is the name of that mountain? Across the valley?" Jurgen asked.

"The Three Sisters," Emma and Carter said at the same time.

"Of course," Jurgen said with a slow nod. "Three peaks. Three sisters."

"My cousins always said those mountains belonged to them," Carter said with a laugh.

"You have cousins?"

"Hailey, Naomi and Shannon," Carter said, pointing to each of the peaks as he listed off his cousins' names.

"The girls all had their own cabin at the ranch, as well," Emma put in. "Those were the cabins you were asking about before Carter joined us."

"So your family spent much time here."

"Whenever we could." More regret twisted his gut. He took a deep breath and struggled to push it aside.

"They did not want to buy this place?" Jurgen asked, pulling his hat off his head, looking over the valley again.

"Couldn't afford it."

"Your price is reasonable."

Carter shrugged. At the time he listed it, he just wanted to be rid of it.

And now?

"Carter isn't a greedy man," Emma said, giving him a quick smile, as if she understood what had gone through his head at the time.

"You two. You don't want to live on this place?" Jurgen's voice held a note of puzzlement.

Emma bit her lip and looked away, and again Carter felt as if he had taken something precious from her. All he could do was slip his arm around her shoulder.

"It is what it is," was all Emma said as she leaned into him, accepting his silent solace.

"Is there anything else you wanted to see?" Carter asked Jurgen, bringing the conversation back to the practical and the immediate.

Jurgen sighed as he worked his hat around his hands. "You two love this place, don't you?"

Emma and Carter locked gazes, sharing a forlorn look.

"I think you do," Jurgen said, answering his own question before Carter formulated a suitable response. "And I think you two care for each other, as well. Have you known each other long?"

Carter shook his head. "We met after I came back to the ranch. About the same time I put the place up for sale."

The only sound that followed his comment was a breeze soughing through the grass, easing away the heat of the sun.

Dusty snorted and Diamond whinnied in response. The horses were growing restless.

"We should probably get back to the ranch," Carter said, turning away and picking up Diamond's reins. He handed them to Jurgen and waited until he and Emma both mounted up before getting on Banjo.

The ride back to the ranch was quiet. Carter was in the lead with Emma bringing up the rear.

As they approached the ranch yard, the horses left behind whinnied. The door of Nana Beck's house flew open and Adam scooted out, running toward the corral to meet them.

Pete, obviously alerted to their presence by Adam's sudden departure, was close behind him. The two of them were waiting when they rode into the corral, Pete standing close to the fence, Adam astride its top beam.

"Did you have a good ride, Mr. Mallik?" Adam called out as they rode by.

"Very nice. Thank you, Adam," Jurgen replied.

"The ranch is really beautiful, isn't it?" Adam added.

"Very beautiful."

"I have a tree fort I could show you. Me and Carter were working on it. But now I won't be able to. 'Cause you're buying the ranch. I'm sad that we can't live here anymore and so is my mommy. She loves it here. Says it's the best home we ever had."

Carter saw Emma frown at Adam and give him a tight shake of her head, as if asking him to stop. Adam got the message and puffed out his cheeks in a sigh of resignation.

"So? What did you think?" Pete asked Jurgen as he slowly dismounted.

"It is a beautiful place. More than beautiful," Jurgen

said as he handed Emma Diamond's halter rope. "But I am of mixed feelings. *Confused,* I think is the word."

"What's to be confused about?" Pete said with a forced laugh, his hands spread out. "The price is perfect. The place is perfect. You've seen it before."

Jurgen scratched his forehead with his index finger, his frown deepening. "I think this is not right, my purchase of this place." He looked over at Carter then toward Emma, who was loosening the cinch of Diamond's saddle with quick, efficient movements.

"What's not right? You did sign all the necessary papers." Pete's voice held a note of warning, and Carter felt tiny pinpricks of apprehension at Pete's concern.

Jurgen sighed and looked over at Carter. "You had a big loss, when your son died here. Then you left and never came back, correct?"

Carter nodded, the pinpricks growing, wondering where Jurgen had gotten this information.

"Your friend Emma told me how sad this made you. While we waited for you earlier," Jurgen said, answering Carter's unspoken question. "But now you seem happy."

Carter's confusion grew. "Yes. I am happy." His gaze drifted toward Emma, who was laughing at something Adam said. As if sensing his regard, she looked his way and, as often happened, an awareness of each other arced between them.

Jurgen followed the direction of his gaze. "This place, you both love it very much."

His voice was matter-of-fact.

"Yes. We do."

"I am thinking you wouldn't choose to sell it now, would you?"

Carter's gaze flew back to Jurgen, a sense of disquiet rising up inside him. "What do you mean?"

"You wanted to wipe away the reminder of your lost son. This was why you wanted to sell. Before you and Emma fall in love." Jurgen's gaze was riveted on Carter, as if trying to delve into Carter's psyche.

Behind him he saw Pete raise his hands in a gesture of surrender.

What was going on?

"Would you sell it now?"

Carter's disquiet morphed into the tiniest beginnings of hope. "No. I wouldn't sell it now."

Jurgen nodded as if that was the answer he was waiting for. Then he looked around the yard, slowly, as if committing each building, each part of the landscape, into memory. "This is a beautiful place with much memory. Much history. I would be happy to own it." Then he looked back at Carter. "But I cannot take this away from you. From Emma and her son. I think this can be a place for you to heal." He turned back to Pete. "I am thinking I want to withdraw my offer. If I am able to. Legally."

"I am thinking you can probably do whatever you want," Pete said in a wry voice, throwing up his hands in a gesture of defeat.

Carter's heart slowed as he tried to absorb what Jurgen was saying.

Jurgen turned back to Carter. "I am hoping you will not sell this place to someone else. But I think you won't."

Carter stared at him, the import of what he said registering word by word.

"You're not buying the place?" was all he could manage, his heart pounding in earnest against his rib cage.

Jurgen shook his head, his mouth curved in a melancholy smile. "I do not want to, how to say, take advantage of your sorrow. I think you are not so sorrowful now." Jurgen extended his hand to Carter.

Carter, still reeling from the shock of what Jurgen had said, could offer only a limp handshake.

"Thanks. Thank you," was all he could stutter out. "Thank you so much."

He stood a moment, surprise and awe rooting him to the spot. Then as everything came together, he said a quick goodbye and ran toward Emma and Adam.

Toward his future.

Chapter Sixteen

"Next time we go on a picnic, I would like to go to the upper pasture," Nana Beck said as she set the cooler down on the blanket Emma had spread out.

It was a glorious Sunday afternoon. When Carter had suggested a family picnic at the old yard site that Emma had, at one time, wanted to buy, she was puzzled but agreed. Then Hailey found out and decided she and Nana would join them.

Though Carter had looked less than impressed, Emma hadn't spent much time with Hailey and looked forward to knowing her better. She seemed spunky and full of fun.

"You have to ride a horse then." Adam dropped down beside the basket, his expression expectant as Nana lifted the lid of the cooler.

"Nana can ride a horse just fine," Hailey said, setting out the plates, her gray eyes flicking from Carter to Emma as if still trying to figure out their relationship. "She taught me how to ride."

"Did she teach you how to snowboard?" Adam asked.

Ever since Adam had seen the broken snowboards in Carter's cabin, he had been curious about the owner.

Carter had obliged by telling him stories of his cousin's many escapades.

"Actually, it was Carter," Hailey said with an exaggerated wink for Emma. "He can shred with the best of them."

"Don't try to pin your kamikaze snowboard routine on me," Carter said with fake indignation as he snapped open a lawn chair. "I didn't even like snowboarding that much."

He set the chair down, and with a wave toward Emma gave a short bow. "Your throne, madam."

"I like how this man thinks," Hailey said with a laugh.

A flush warmed Emma's face as Carter bent over to place a kiss on her cheeks. He touched her nose with his finger and winked at her. "Have a seat, my dear."

Behind the flush came a rush of love so complete, so full, it threatened to overwhelm her. She wasn't so independent that she didn't like having a man fuss over her from time to time. "Thanks. I think I will."

Carter brought over a second chair to her grandmother, and as she sat down Nana Beck looked around, her smile wide with pleasure. "Isn't this nice. Too bad Shannon couldn't join us."

"Cluck, cluck," Hailey said with a laugh as she dropped down on the blanket beside Adam. "Nana won't be happy until all her little chicks come home to roost."

"Where they belong," Nana said. "But for now I am so grateful to God that three of my chicks are back in Hartley Creek. And that Jurgen changed his mind about buying the ranch. I prayed for a miracle, but I didn't think it would come this way."

Carter sat down beside Emma and laid his hand on her knee. "It was a miracle," he agreed. "And I'm thankful for it."

"No such things as miracles," Hailey said, her voice taking on a surprisingly tough edge.

"Oh, yes, there are," Nana said, patting Hailey on the shoulder. "You'll see. Someday."

Hailey's only answer was a light shrug.

Emma leaned back in the chair, unwilling to let Hailey's little negative comment ruin the moment for her. The sun shone like a blessing on the moment, and Adam was happier than she'd seen him in months.

As for herself, she sat beside the man she loved.

"Ironic that you picked this place to have a picnic," Hailey said to Carter. "Wasn't this the homestead Emma wanted you to subdivide for her?"

"It was."

"So why did you want us to have the picnic here?"

"I planned a picnic for just her and me and Adam. And I wanted to have it here because I wanted to bring things full circle."

"What are you talking about?" Hailey asked.

Carter scratched the side of his nose, then pulled his hat off and laid it to one side.

"Uh-oh. I see a serious face," Hailey said.

Carter laid his finger over his lips. "To everything there is a season, and now is the time for quiet. You weren't supposed to be here, so pretend, for the next few moments, like you're not."

Hailey frowned, and as Carter pulled out two tiny boxes from his shirt pocket, Emma felt her heart quicken.

She hardly dared breathe. Hardly dared let her mind go too far ahead.

Carter turned to her and, to her amazement, got down on one knee.

Emma looked down into Carter's gentle blue eyes,

wondering why she had ever thought them cold when they shone with such warmth now.

"I think I like where this is going," Hailey whispered to Adam.

"Where is it going?" he whispered back.

"Wait and see," Nana said. "Hush, now."

Carter took her hand in his and everything and everyone else faded away until it was just Carter and her.

"Emma, I love you. More than I ever thought I could love a person again." Emma's heart tripped in her chest at the expression of devotion on his face. He opened the first box. Inside she saw the wink of a diamond, and tears threatened.

"Emma Minton, will you marry me?"

She nodded, blinking away her tears.

Then she was in his arms, his mouth pressed against hers, and a faint breeze picked up and swirled around them like a benediction.

Her heart felt like bursting, and she couldn't hold him close enough, couldn't be held close enough.

"Thank You, Lord," she whispered in Carter's ear.

She drew back, and Carter slipped the ring on her finger. The diamond winked in the sun, like a promise.

"I love you, Emma," he said, his voice breaking. "And I'll try to be worthy of the trust you said you placed in me." Carter turned her hand over and pressed a kiss to her palm, as if sealing that promise.

"I love you too," she said, her voice breaking. "I love you so much." It was all she could say.

"Is that where this is going?" Adam asked.

Carter turned to Adam and gestured for him to come over. Adam scrambled to his feet and ran over. Carter caught him in a one-armed hug and pulled him close. Adam pointed. "What's in that box?"

"Let's see," Carter replied. He let go of Adam.

Carter opened the other box and pulled out a golden necklace. From it dangled the gold pendant Emma had seen shortly after Carter had come back to the ranch. "You were there when Nana told the story about this pendant," Carter said quietly, unclasping the necklace. "I want you to have this as a reminder of the choices my grandfather made. And as a reminder that you are now part of this family. Woven into the stories and the legends."

He placed the necklace around Emma's neck and kissed her again.

"I love a happy ending," Hailey said in a choked voice.

"I do too," Nana replied.

"Is this the end of the picnic?" Adam asked sadly.

"No, Adam. It's just the beginning." Carter pulled Emma close and wrapped Adam into the three-way embrace.

Emma returned the hug, trying to take it all in. Trying to absorb that she and Adam were now a part of Carter's life, present and future.

As he drew away, her eyes flitted from Adam to Hailey to Nana Beck, her heart full of love, joy. And below all that, a comforting thread of peace.

This was a homecoming.

She and Carter and Adam—they had all found home.

* * * * *

Dear Reader,

I had a hard time finding the right emotional tone for this book, because losing a child is such a heart-rending experience. As my grandmother said, to bury parents is the normal flow of life and death. To bury a child goes against every part of our nature. She knew what she spoke about. She buried three. When I wrote this book, I wanted to be true to what a parent experiences when a child is lost and yet hold out hope that the pain does shift. The edges wear off. It doesn't go away, but after a while you don't mind living with the sorrow.

Eighteen years ago, my family followed the small coffin of our son out of our church and into the adjoining graveyard and watched it being lowered into the earth. The pain did ease off and the sorrow lost its bite. And through it all, our family felt the prayers of the community and the strength of God's abiding and unfailing love.

Carter had to learn to let people into his life so that he could share his pain and, by sharing it, lose some of the burden of it. I pray, if you have suffered a deep loss, that you too will know that even in the storm, God is there, holding you. I pray you will feel the prayers of the people around you and let them hold you too.

Carolyne Aarsen

P.S. I love to hear from my readers. Send me a note at caarsen@xplornet.com, or stop by my website www.carolyneaarsen.com. On my website, be sure to check out the *Hartley Creek Herald* for news about happenings in and around Hartley Creek.

Questions for Discussion

1. One of the statements that is repeated in this book is "Peace is not the absence of trouble, peace is the presence of God." How do you feel about that statement?

2. Has this been true for your life? If so, how?

3. Why do you think Carter struggled with so much guilt over his son's death when he wasn't even on the ranch when it happened?

4. As a parent, we always want to protect our children. How does this show in Emma's relationship with Adam?

5. I have discovered that so many parents struggle with guilt over various things they have done to their children. I know I do. Why do you think that is?

6. Emma felt she couldn't trust men again. Do you think she was justified in feeling that way? Why, or why not?

7. Have you or someone you know ever experienced a loss like Carter's? How did you cope, if it was your loss? How did you extend comfort if it was someone else's?

8. How can we help people who lose a child?

9. Emma and Carter both loved the ranch. What did the ranch represent to each of them?

10. Have you had times when you didn't feel God near to you? What did you do?

11. Carter's grandmother gave him a nugget and a Bible. What did they represent to his grandmother, and what did they mean to him?

12. What was your reaction to Carter and Emma's relationship? Did it ring true? Why or why not?

13. What changes did they have to make in their lives to accommodate each other?

INSPIRATIONAL

Inspirational romances to warm your heart & soul.

TITLES AVAILABLE NEXT MONTH

Available September 27, 2011

THE CHRISTMAS CHILD
Redemption River
Linda Goodnight

THE COWBOY'S LADY
Rocky Mountain Heirs
Carolyne Aarsen

ANNA'S GIFT
Hannah's Daughters
Emma Miller

BUILDING A FAMILY
New Friends Street
Lyn Cote

HEALING AUTUMN'S HEART
Renee Andrews

OKLAHOMA REUNION
Tina Radcliffe

LICNM0911

REQUEST YOUR FREE BOOKS!

2 FREE INSPIRATIONAL NOVELS
PLUS 2
FREE
MYSTERY GIFTS

YES! Please send me 2 FREE Love Inspired® novels and my 2 FREE mystery gifts (gifts are worth about $10). After receiving them, if I don't wish to receive any more books, I can return the shipping statement marked "cancel." If I don't cancel, I will receive 6 brand-new novels every month and be billed just $4.49 per book in the U.S. or $4.99 per book in Canada. That's a saving of at least 22% off the cover price. It's quite a bargain! Shipping and handling is just 50¢ per book in the U.S. and 75¢ per book in Canada.* I understand that accepting the 2 free books and gifts places me under no obligation to buy anything. I can always return a shipment and cancel at any time. Even if I never buy another book, the two free books and gifts are mine to keep forever.

105/305 IDN FEGR

Name	(PLEASE PRINT)

Address	Apt. #

City	State/Prov.	Zip/Postal Code

Signature (if under 18, a parent or guardian must sign)

Mail to the **Reader Service:**
IN U.S.A.: P.O. Box 1867, Buffalo, NY 14240-1867
IN CANADA: P.O. Box 609, Fort Erie, Ontario L2A 5X3

Not valid for current subscribers to Love Inspired books.

**Are you a subscriber to Love Inspired books
and want to receive the larger-print edition?
Call 1-800-873-8635 or visit www.ReaderService.com.**

* Terms and prices subject to change without notice. Prices do not include applicable taxes. Sales tax applicable in N.Y. Canadian residents will be charged applicable taxes. Offer not valid in Quebec. This offer is limited to one order per household. All orders subject to credit approval. Credit or debit balances in a customer's account(s) may be offset by any other outstanding balance owed by or to the customer. Please allow 4 to 6 weeks for delivery. Offer available while quantities last.

Your Privacy—The Reader Service is committed to protecting your privacy. Our Privacy Policy is available online at www.ReaderService.com or upon request from the Reader Service.

We make a portion of our mailing list available to reputable third parties that offer products we believe may interest you. If you prefer that we not exchange your name with third parties, or if you wish to clarify or modify your communication preferences, please visit us at www.ReaderService.com/consumerschoice or write to us at Reader Service Preference Service, P.O. Box 9062, Buffalo, NY 14269. Include your complete name and address.

LIREG11B

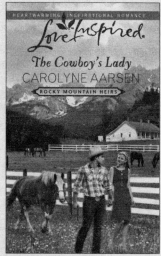